An excerpt from KID

As soon as the door to OR Room 6 closed behind them, Connor turned to Cassie. "Follow me."

He opened a narrow door nearby and led Cassie up some steps and into a small observation room. Connor sat on one of the small yellow plastic chairs lined up along the window. Cassie sat next to him, and they both stared into the OR.

"I've never lost a patient … before today," Connor said.

Cassie's mouth dropped open with surprise. "Really? I thought that people die all the time in the ER."

"Not at Westley Hospital," Connor said. "Have *you* ever lost a patient?"

"Two. At the same time. The mother's uterus ruptured. Both she and the baby died." She swallowed hard and then continued, her voice weak, "When your patients die, I think little pieces of you die too."

"What happens when you run out of pieces?" Connor asked.

"I don't know."

Praise for KID DOCS

"Five stars. Amazing! I am actually speechless because it was so good. I would read it over again. I recommend this book to anyone." - Shelby, Goodreads

"I'm ready for more! A five star book EASY!"
- Pepper, Goodreads

"Intriguing. Incredibly engaging. I highly recommend this book. It's definitely a read you won't forget." - Amy, Goodreads

"The hospital setting was rich and accurate, with enough medical details to pique the curiosity of kids who might be so inclined, or to feed the fascination of adults who like to watch medical shows. I always appreciate dramatic suspense in a novel, and this one had it. Plenty of plot points kept me reading: finding out how the kid docs will react to the pressure, the fate of the patients who come into the hospital, and even the fate of one of their own."
- Jennifer Donovan, 5 Minutes for Books

KID DOCS

J.W. LYNNE

This book is a work of fiction. Names, characters, places, organizations, programs, businesses, incidents, etc. either are products of the author's imagination or are used fictitiously. Any resemblance to actual persons, living or dead, events, organizations, programs, businesses, locales, etc. is entirely coincidental.

Copyright © 2012 by J.W. Lynne
All rights reserved.

Except as permitted under the U.S. Copyright Act of 1976, no part of this publication may be reproduced, distributed, or transmitted in any form or by any means, or stored in a database or retrieval system, without the prior written permission of the author.

ISBN 978-1482008692

To Matthew, Wyatt, Luke, Jordan, Cameron, Lily, Amelia, Caitlyn, Madeline, Jackson, Zachary, Blake, Addison, Noella, and Keegan.

KID DOCS

Chapter One

Fourteen-year-old Connor Hansen raced at full speed through the shiny, sterile emergency room hallways of Westley Hospital. He was excited ... and terrified. He was about to do what he had been training for almost his entire life. But if he failed, someone would die. Paramedics rushed toward him, pushing a bright-yellow gurney that carried a bloodied, lifeless man whose heart had stopped beating. It was Connor's job to get the man's heart started again. Connor was a doctor.

One of the paramedics pushed down on the patient's chest with both hands, again and again, attempting to pump blood through the man's body. The other paramedic occasionally squeezed a balloon-like resuscitation bag, filling the man's lungs with oxygen.

As he ran up to the paramedics, Connor quietly took an uncertain breath and asked the question he'd been taught to ask, "What have we got?"

One of the paramedics responded with an answer

that sounded like gibberish, "Forty-two-year-old male status post MVA. In v-fib at the scene. Converted to sinus rhythm after defibrillation. Went back into v-fib when we were pulling up to your door."

Connor understood every word.

His patient had been in a car accident. When the paramedics arrived at the scene of the accident, the man's heart was quivering helplessly, unable to pump blood to his body. The paramedics had sent a powerful jolt of electricity through the man's chest that made his heart start beating again. But moments ago, in the ambulance, the heart had begun quivering again. The man's heart was dying. Connor couldn't let that happen.

The paramedics slid the man onto the skinny, padded table in the center of Trauma Room One. Connor took his place on the stepstool that was waiting for him. Although he was about to do a man's job, he didn't feel like a man. He didn't look much like a man either. His muscles were still small and undeveloped, and he had only recently started his growth spurt.

Connor shouted out instructions to the doctors and nurses surrounding the table: blood and urine tests to perform, x-ray pictures to take. But that was where the easy part of his job ended. Now Connor had to get this man's heart beating again. Every minute that passed made success less and less likely.

Connor had become a doctor just two days ago—along with all of his friends. They were hand-selected at just three years old to undergo intensive medical training as part of a controversial experiment, called Kid Docs. In the past few years, the Kid Docs program had produced some of the best doctors in the entire country, if not the world. They had some of the lowest complication rates and the highest success rates, and they had developed innovative new procedures that saved lives that were previously unsalvageable. Connor hoped that he would be among the best doctors in the world someday. But right now, he was focused on only a single thing: saving this one man's life.

As the paramedics ran toward the door with their empty gurney, Connor asked them, "What's the patient's name?"

"Peterson," one of the paramedics responded. "Eric Peterson."

Hearing that name made an awful feeling rise in Connor's chest. His gaze fell to his patient's bruised face, and then his gut twisted in horror. His hands became even sweatier inside his rubber gloves than they had been before.

He knew this man.

Connor tried to focus. He listened to Mr. Peterson's lungs as Brandon—a plump, olive-skinned medical student who was two years younger than Connor—squeezed the resuscitation bag attached to the mask that was pressed against Mr. Peterson's face. Connor touched his fingers to Mr. Peterson's neck where he felt blood pulsing through an artery whenever Hannah—an ER doctor who was the same age as Connor—pumped blood through Mr. Peterson's body by bearing down on his chest with her hands, over and over, using all of the force she could muster.

"Hold CPR for a rhythm check," Connor ordered his team.

Hannah immediately followed Connor's instructions, lifting her hands from Mr. Peterson's chest. Brandon removed the mask from Mr. Peterson's face and looked wide-eyed at Connor, awaiting further instructions. Connor avoided Brandon's searching eyes. When he was Brandon's age, Connor thought ER doctors were extremely mature and confident. Now that he was an ER doctor himself, he didn't feel mature or confident at all, but it was his responsibility to make his team feel that they were in capable hands.

Connor placed his fingers back on Mr. Peterson's neck. Since Hannah was no longer pressing on their patient's chest, Connor no longer felt the reassuring pulsing of blood. His fingers detected no signs of life at all. The heart monitor connected to his patient showed a wild zigzagging line. Mr. Peterson's heart was still quivering rather than beating.

Connor's body tensed with concern. "V-fib. Resume CPR."

Hannah began rhythmically pushing on Mr. Peterson's chest again, her forehead wrinkled with exertion as she desperately tried to pump blood through their patient's dying body.

Connor ordered the defibrillator machine to be readied, "Charge to two hundred." He was going to send a jolt of electricity through Mr. Peterson's body, just like the paramedics had done. He didn't know if this would start the heart beating again, but it might. Connor involuntarily held his breath. He hoped this would work. He needed this to work. Mr. Peterson was running out of time.

"Charging," Nurse Samantha said. She was one of the few adults on Connor's team. She towered over the doctors and medical students, even though the doctors and medical students stood on stepstools. Her long brown hair was woven into two neat braids that fell down her back. She always wore her hair that way. It made her look like a grown-up-sized kid. Of all the nurses in the ER, Nurse Samantha was one of Connor's favorites. She treated him with the kind of respect that most adults only show to other adults.

Nurse Samantha stood beside the defibrillator that sat atop the fire-engine-red medical supply cart next to Mr. Peterson's bed. The defibrillator was emitting a long, loud, high-pitched, awful sound. Connor grabbed its paddles, and Nurse Samantha squirted some special green jelly onto them. Then Connor pressed their cold metal plates against Mr. Peterson's bare chest.

"Clear," Connor shouted, making his voice sound strong and steady, the exact opposite of what he was feeling inside. He pushed red buttons that had lightning-bolt symbols on them, releasing the shock.

Mr. Peterson's body jerked, as if he were a life-sized rag-doll shook by an invisible giant. The line on the heart monitor shot up and then down ... and then it started zigzagging again.

The shock hadn't worked.

Everyone sprang back into action. Except Connor. He just stared at his patient, feeling hot and numb. He couldn't think straight.

"Connor?" Hannah whispered.

Connor wondered whether she could tell that he was freaking out. He figured she probably could. Hannah and Connor had been best friends for so long that sometimes it seemed as if they were able to read each other's minds.

Examine your patient, he could almost hear Hannah say inside his head as she stared at him with tough, determined eyes.

Connor did as she "told him" and checked Mr. Peterson's belly, gently pressing against it with his trembling fingertips. It was rock hard.

"Abdomen's rigid," Connor reported. "He's bleeding internally. We're gonna need lots of blood?" He glanced around the room taking in the controlled chaos of nurses and doctors, all performing their tasks. "Shouldn't trauma surgery be here by now?" he asked.

"Surgery's on their way," Nurse Samantha said, hanging a bulging bag of red-purple blood on an IV pole.

Connor moved his attention down to his patient's splinted legs. Both thighs were swollen and misshapen. He didn't need an x-ray to know that Mr. Peterson's thighbones were broken. It takes a lot of force to break a femur.

Connor's head felt foggy again. *What if Mr. Peterson is too injured to survive?* Connor's heart pounded furiously against his ribcage. *No!* he told himself, pushing the negative thoughts from his brain. *Mr. Peterson is going to be fine. He has to be.*

"I'm gonna intubate," Connor shouted over the voices of the other medical personnel. He kicked his stepstool closer to the head of the table and grabbed a laryngoscope—a metal flashlight with a long silver blade protruding from one end. Connor slid the laryngoscope blade deep into Mr. Peterson's mouth. Muscling the patient's heavy tongue and jaw out of his way, Connor slipped the tip of the blade all the way down into the man's throat. Nurse Samantha placed a plastic breathing tube in Connor's other hand. Carefully, he threaded the tube between vocal cords that looked like parted, pink curtains.

Brandon attached the resuscitation bag to the end

of the breathing tube and then squeezed the bag as Nurse Samantha listened to Mr. Peterson's chest.

"Breath sounds equal," Nurse Samantha said.

Hannah turned to Connor and smiled. "Great job, Connor!"

But there was no time for Connor to enjoy his success. As far as he knew, Mr. Peterson's heart still wasn't beating.

"Rhythm check," Connor barked out.

Hannah stopped pressing on the patient's chest, and Connor checked the heart monitor. The bad zigzagging line was *still* on its screen. Connor's stomach sunk.

"V-fib," he said. "Give him epi and charge to three hundred."

Nurse Samantha turned a dial on the defibrillator and pressed a button. The machine emitted its awful squeal.

Another nurse—a serious-looking woman wearing glasses—emptied two syringes full of clear liquid into Mr. Peterson's IV tube, and then shouted, "Epi's in."

Connor placed the metal defibrillator paddles onto Mr. Peterson's chest once again. "Clear." He pressed the lightning bolt buttons, and Mr. Peterson's body jerked unnaturally for an instant. On the heart monitor, the zigzagging line shot up and then down ... and then it became *flat*.

Mr. Peterson's heart wasn't quivering anymore. It had completely stopped. Connor felt like his own heart might stop.

"Resume CPR," Connor said through the lump in this throat.

But just before Hannah's gloved hands touched Mr. Peterson's chest, the heart monitor let out a soft bleep.

Then another bleep.

Then another bleep.

Connor's gaze flew to the monitor. Little blips appeared in the line running across the screen.

"Sinus rhythm," Connor said in thrilled disbelief.

Hannah placed her fingers on Mr. Peterson's neck. "He's got a pulse!" she announced, grinning with excitement.

Mr. Peterson's heart was finally beating!

Applause broke out in a corner of the trauma room. A few adults emerged from the shadows led by a slim, blond-haired man who looked like a much older version of Connor. He was Connor's dad, Doctor

Mark Hansen.

"Nice work, everyone!" Connor's dad said. And then he leaned close to Connor and added, "Excellent job, Connor."

Connor's dad rarely smiled, but he was smiling right now. Connor could tell that his dad was really proud of him. But there was something about this patient that his dad didn't know. Something Connor knew would change his dad's pride to shame.

Nurse Mike—whose broad shoulders made him look like he belonged on a football field rather than in an ER—burst through the door. "Mr. Peterson's wife is here. Want me to bring her in?"

Connor didn't answer, even through it was obvious that Nurse Mike was speaking to him.

"I'll go talk to her," Hannah volunteered.

"Thanks," Connor mumbled.

Hannah looked at him. "You all right?" she whispered.

"Yeah," Connor lied, and then he turned his focus back to his patient.

* * *

Connor had to walk at more than triple his normal

speed to keep pace with Mr. Peterson's gurney as it moved down the hallway, away from the ER. Two trauma surgeons—who were one year older than Connor—wheeled the gurney. The surgeons had taken over Mr. Peterson's care. They were planning to bring the patient to the operating room, cut open his belly, and attempt to repair his damaged organs.

Even though Mr. Peterson was no longer Connor's responsibility, Connor still felt responsible for him. As the surgeons boarded the elevator with their patient, Connor recited Mr. Peterson's most recent lab results and then added, "If you have any questions, just call me."

"Don't worry," the female surgeon said. "We'll take good care of him." She barely glanced at Connor as the elevator doors closed.

Connor was left all alone in the ER hallway. His stomach remained sick with anxiety. *If Mr. Peterson dies, it will be all my fault,* he thought.

He started away from the elevator in a daze, hardly looking where he was going, and nearly collided with a fast-moving doctor coming the opposite way.

"Excuse me," the doctor said with a bright smile,

her blue eyes beaming at his. Fiery-red, wavy hair cascaded down her shoulders. She appeared to be about Connor's age, but he didn't recall having met her before.

"It was my fault," Connor apologized, looking down at his feet.

She offered her hand. "I'm Cassie Blum, obstetrics."

Connor politely took hold of her hand for a moment. It was so warm and comforting that, after he let it go, he wished he could hold it again. "Connor Hansen, emergency medicine." His voice cracked when he spoke. He cringed. He hated it when his voice did that.

Cassie didn't seem to notice or care about Connor's voice. She smiled again. "You're Doctor Hansen's kid."

"One of them," Connor mumbled. Then he tried to change the subject, "Is someone delivering a baby down here?"

"Yup," she replied, and then her smile widened and her eyebrows rose as if she had a brilliant idea. "Hey, have you ever seen a childbirth?"

Connor shook his head. "No."

"Wanna come?"

Before Connor could answer that he did not, Cassie took him by the arm and led him into a room where a heavily-perspiring woman alternately panted and screamed. The woman appeared to be in a lot of pain. A man wearing rumpled gym clothes stood by her side, holding a wet washcloth to her forehead. His tight brow made him look as bewildered as Connor felt. Connor assumed the man was the woman's husband.

Cassie pulled on a blue paper gown and a pair of sterile rubber gloves while she studied the pulsating graphs of data on a computer monitor. "Mrs. Harris, you're doing great!" she told the perspiring woman.

Mrs. Harris doesn't look like she's doing great at all, Connor thought. His instinct was to help this patient, but he wasn't sure what to do. At the Kid Docs program, students are tested when they are five years old to determine the area of medicine they will focus on, then they are trained only in that specialty. While Connor knew a lot about emergency medicine, he knew almost nothing about delivering babies. He felt like he was an insecure, inexperienced seventh year medical student again—just starting to help care for patients in the hospital.

"Sandra, gown and glove Doctor Connor too, please," Cassie told the squat, stout nurse who was standing by the patient's feet.

Fear rose in Connor's chest. "Why?" he asked. He wasn't planning to touch the patient. If he was merely going to *watch* a baby be born, he shouldn't need to wear a gown or gloves.

"You're going to catch," Cassie replied.

"What's your glove size, Doctor Connor?" Nurse Sandra asked as she squirted some water-free cleanser onto his hands.

"Six and a half," he answered reflexively. Immediately, he regretted answering. He wanted to excuse himself and leave, but he was fast becoming a participant in whatever was about to happen here.

"Perfect," Nurse Sandra said to him, opening a package of sterile gloves. "Same size as Doctor Cassie."

For some reason that he couldn't determine, Connor's cheeks burned with embarrassment at the fact that his hands were exactly the same size as this girl's.

Nurse Sandra pushed a paper gown over Connor's

arms and up onto his shoulders, then she slipped rubber gloves onto his hands.

"Baby's head's out. No more pushing, Mrs. Harris," Cassie said to the patient in a firm, but reassuring, voice.

Connor's curiosity pulled his gaze in the same direction as Cassie's. He felt his eyes widen as he caught sight of the baby's head. It was an ominous purple-blue color.

"Why is the head *purple*?" Connor whispered to Cassie, trying to sound professional but coming across a little panicked.

"Because the baby hasn't started breathing yet," she said. Cassie took Connor's freshly-gloved hands and placed them on the tiny purple head. Even through two layers of rubber, Cassie's hands still felt soothing.

"What do you want me to do?" Connor asked, trying to keep his tone relaxed and normal-sounding.

"Just hold onto the head for me," she said, with the slightest hint of tension in her voice. "The cord is wrapped around the baby's neck. I need to unwrap it." Connor looked at where Cassie pointed. A thick, rope-like thing was wound tightly around the baby's neck. It appeared as if the baby was being strangled by it.

Cassie eased her fingers under the cord, gently pulling it away from the baby. Connor watched in amazement as, ever so slowly, little by little, the thing loosened its grip. Cassie slid the slackened cord up over the baby's head, freeing the child, but the baby didn't start to breathe and the infant's skin remained disturbingly purple.

Cassie put her hands back on top of Connor's. "Now a little downward traction. Then up." As she spoke, she guided Connor's hands—and the baby's head—down and then up.

The baby shot into Connor's arms as if it had exploded from a cannon. He hugged the slippery infant to his chest, like he would if he were catching a slimy, fragile football. Cassie kept a protective grip on the baby, and so, when the newborn rested securely in Connor's arms, Cassie and Connor stood face-to-face. Her gaze met his for an instant, before they both looked down at the child.

"It's a boy!" Cassie announced to everyone in the room, without taking her attention off the newborn. The baby was silent, motionless, and still ominously purple. He appeared ... dead.

Cassie used a small, blue device that fit in the

palm of her hand to suction fluid from the baby's mouth and nostrils, but the infant showed no response to her interventions. "Come on, little man," she said as she vigorously rubbed his back. "Take a big breath for me."

Suddenly, as if triggered by magic, the baby let out a piercing wail, and the infant's face flushed with healthy, pink-red color. Connor felt himself exhale. He hadn't realized that he'd been holding his breath.

The newborn squirmed in Connor's arms as Nurse Sandra dried the child and wrapped him in a warm blanket. Connor stared at the baby, in shock over what he'd just witnessed.

"Go ahead and give the baby to his mommy," Cassie whispered to Connor.

Connor walked to the head of the bed and carefully placed the baby into Mrs. Harris's waiting arms. The new mother kissed her infant on the forehead as tears flowed down her cheeks. Mr. Harris cried too as he lightly stroked his tiny son's fingers and spoke to him softly. The baby stopped crying, and he gazed into his father's tear-filled eyes.

Connor looked at his bloody gown. It was quite possibly the bloodiest gown he'd ever worn, and yet both of the patients he'd just treated were now perfectly fine and so very happy. Feeling pleased with himself, Connor pulled off his soiled gown and gloves and deposited them in the trash.

When he glanced up, Connor saw Cassie looking at him looking as if she was fighting back a smile. He wanted to smile back at her, but instead, feeling awkward, he looked away.

* * *

"What are you doing after work?" Cassie asked Connor as they left Mrs. Harris's room a few minutes later.

Connor shrugged. "I don't know."

Usually Connor went home when his hospital shift was over, but today he didn't feel like going home. He didn't want to face his dad, even though his dad likely had no idea why.

"Wanna do something?" Cassie asked.

"Like what?" As soon as he said that, Connor had an idea. "Hey, I know what we can do!"

"What?" Cassie asked, her eyes gleaming with curiosity.

"Let's meet in the first floor doctors' lounge at

five-thirty …" Connor didn't want to tell Cassie the rest of his plans just yet. What he wanted to do with her was against the rules. He'd have to decide first if she could be trusted.

Before he could figure out what to say next, Connor's pager beeped. His jaw clenched as he remembered that he was supposed to be giving a tour of Westley Hospital to the parents of a prospective student at that very moment. He was already ten minutes late.

"I've gotta go," Connor said to Cassie. "See ya at five-thirty?"

"Yeah, okay. See ya," she said, her eyes narrowed with amused suspicion.

Connor rushed to the elevator. He pushed the call button a few times, even though he knew doing that wouldn't make the elevator come any faster. When the elevator arrived, he took it to the fourteenth floor, where he hopped off and walked quickly to his dad's office.

Inside the office, he found his dad's assistant, Jennifer, talking with a man and a woman. They all wore crisp business suits that contrasted sharply with Connor's puke-green, pajama-like doctor scrubs.

"Sorry I'm late," Connor apologized to everyone.

"No worries," Jennifer responded pleasantly, as she always did.

Connor had known Jennifer since before he could remember. She was the closest person to a mother that he had in his life. His real mother died when he was just a few months old.

Jennifer handed Connor a sheet of paper listing the information he would need for the tour. He quickly skimmed it. The man and woman were Mr. and Mrs. Mather. The Mathers' three-year-old daughter, Carolyn, had shown an exceptionally high aptitude toward surgery on her preliminary testing. Carolyn had the potential to be a huge asset to the Kid Docs program. Her application had been triple-starred. Triple-starred applications were extremely rare.

When they first arrive at Westley Hospital, most parents of prospective students are initially skeptical. Despite what they've seen on TV and read in newspapers and magazines, they usually don't fully believe that the Kid Docs program will be able to properly prepare their child to be a happy, well-adjusted, successful doctor. Connor's role in the tour was to eliminate their doubts.

"Let's get going," Connor said to the Mathers.

The man and woman stood and followed him out the door. As soon as the door closed behind them, Mrs. Mather turned to Connor. "How old are you?" Her question sounded more like an accusation than normal conversation.

Connor stiffened. "I'm fourteen."

"And you're an *actual* doctor?" Mr. Mather asked.

"Yes," Connor said as he headed toward the elevators.

"How could you possibly have enough experience to be responsible for people's lives?" Mrs. Mather asked, her high-heeled shoes clicking on the floor as she hurried after him.

Before Connor could answer, Mr. Mather added, "What if a patient has a problem that you've never treated before and you aren't sure what to do?"

Connor swallowed back the tension rising in his chest. He pressed the elevator call button, and one of the elevators promptly opened. The Mathers followed Connor inside. When he turned around, they were facing him. He felt cornered, like a small animal trapped by its predators.

Connor took a breath and began to answer the questions that had been posed to him, "Before I became a doctor, I spent ten years as a medical student. I spent four of those years in the hospital, assisting other doctors. Now I see patients independently, but there's always an adult doctor immediately available if I have any questions about what to do, and a supervising doctor reviews my charts within twenty-four hours." For the first time, Connor noticed a flaw in way the Kid Docs are supervised: what if, when he was treating a patient, he didn't ask the right questions? He could make a mistake that might not be noticed until hours later. By then, it might be too late.

Before the Mathers could ask any further questions, Connor continued, "We're now heading to the operating room to see Doctor Alex Hansen treating a patient who was born with a defect in the wall of the heart and coarctation of the aorta." Alex was Connor's older brother. He was one of the first kids to be enrolled in the Kid Docs program. Two years ago, when he was fourteen years old, Alex became the youngest heart surgeon in the world.

"What's coarctation of the aorta?" Mr. Mather

asked.

"It's a condition where the large blood vessel that carries blood from the heart to the body is too narrow. The surgeon can either cut out the narrowed portion and sew the ends back together or enlarge the area using a patch."

The elevator doors opened, and Connor led Mr. and Mrs. Mather to an OR prep room. After they washed their hands, Connor handed them each a pair of oversized white coveralls and explained, "This is a bunny suit. Guests to the OR wear these in order to prevent germs from entering the operating rooms." The bunny suits completely covered their clothes and zipped up the front.

After everyone was properly dressed in their bunny suits, Connor helped Mr. and Mrs. Mather put on puffy pale-blue shoe covers, tuck their hair inside poofy shower-cap-like hats, and secure surgical masks over their mouths and noses. Then he quickly put on his own shoe covers, hat, and mask. The only parts of their bodies that remained visible were their hands, necks, and a small portion of their faces.

Connor led the Mathers to OR Four. As Connor pushed open the metal door, the circulating nurse—

one of only two adults inside the operating room—acknowledged them. Alex and the three other Kid Docs huddled over the operating table were so intensely focused on their work that they didn't notice that anyone had arrived.

The Mathers stared at the tiny chest that had been cut open in order to repair the malformed heart and blood vessel. The little heart wasn't moving and the lungs weren't inflating. In the ER, this would be a terrible sign, a sign that the patient was dead, but Alex and his team had everything under control. The patient's blood was coursing through clear tubes that led to a heart-lung machine, which added oxygen and removed carbon dioxide before it sent the blood back to the patient's body. Near the head of the operating table was the anesthesiologist—Trevor, a Kid Doc who was one year ahead of Connor. Trevor was in charge of keeping the patient alive while the surgeons worked.

"The patient is just a child," Mrs. Mather whispered to her husband, her eyes widened with horror.

"We treat people of all ages," Connor said in a hushed voice.

"Don't the child's parents have to consent to that?" Mr. Mather asked, incredulous.

"Yes," Connor said.

"I wouldn't let *experimental* doctors operate on *my* child," Mrs. Mather said.

"Absolutely not," Mr. Mather concurred.

Connor felt his face burn with indignation. "Doctor Alex is one of the top heart surgeons in the country. He has saved the lives of countless patients who adult surgeons deemed too high-risk to undergo surgical treatment. Doctors from Japan, England, Australia, and all kinds of places come to Westley Hospital to learn techniques that Alex pioneered. Any patient would be fortunate to—"

"Shhh," one of the nurses hissed.

Connor was grateful. The Mathers would have to be quiet now too, at least until they left the operating room.

The steady hum of machines harmonized with Alex's voice. "Pull up. Cut. Pull up. Cut. Suction." He held out a gloved hand toward the nurse who stood next to him. "Paddles."

Alex was ready to restart the patient's heart.

The nurse handed Alex two rods that had thick

rubber grips at one end and flat metal spoons at the other. They reminded Connor of salad tongs. Alex slid the spoon ends into his patient's chest, placing one spoon on either side of the little heart.

Mr. Mather's shoulders tensed. Mrs. Mather's forehead creased with worry.

"Here we go." Alex pressed a red button on the grip of one of the sticks, jolting the heart with a burst of electricity. Immediately, it came alive, rhythmically contracting as if nothing at all had ever happened to it. As if it had never stopped beating.

Mrs. Mather watched the little heart pump, tears pooling in her eyes. "Incredible!" she breathed.

Alex passed the paddles back to the nurse, glanced at the tallest of the other three Kid Docs surgeons, and said, "Alyson, you close." Without waiting for her response, he pulled off his gown and gloves and left the room without saying another word.

As Connor led the Mathers out of the OR, Mrs. Mather wiped tears from her cheeks. "How old are those doctors?" she asked, her tone more curious than accusatory.

"Alex is the oldest. He's sixteen," Connor said. "Alyson is fifteen. The two surgical medical students are eleven or twelve, I think. And the anesthesiologist … he's fifteen."

"How do they teach you to do all this?" Mr. Mather asked, shaking his head in disbelief.

"I'll show you," Connor said.

* * *

Connor swiped his ID badge at the back entrance of Kid Docs School—an unpretentious brick building in the shadow of towering, shimmering Westley Hospital. The door popped open, admitting Connor and the Mathers to the school's main hallway. Large, brightly-colored bulletin boards displayed children's artwork like that seen in a typical school—aside from the fact that these paintings and collages featured detailed images of the heart, brain, and other organs of the human body. Connor directed the Mathers forward, and the three of them started down the hallway.

"Doctor Connor, do you feel you've received a well-rounded education?" Mrs. Mather asked, reverting to the interrogating tone she'd used earlier. "I mean, did you learn about the government and politics? Have you studied geography? History?"

Connor took a breath, trying to squelch the hot

frustration percolating up his spine. He was accustomed to people questioning him, testing him. Usually, he liked the challenge. But right now it bothered him, although he wasn't sure why.

"We are educated in a variety of subjects," Connor said. "We're also invited to attend enrichment classes and cultural events that suit our interests, and we have unlimited access to a full digital library of books and movies."

"What year did the Second World War start?" Mr. Mather quizzed.

Instead of answering the question, Connor asked, "How would you calculate the dose of epinephrine for a child whose throat is swelling shut due to anaphylactic shock? Can you recite the algorithm for resuscitating a person in cardiac arrest? What is the first thing you would do if a person's lung ruptures and their chest is filling with air, compressing their heart and compromising their breathing?"

The Mathers stared at him blankly.

Connor smirked. "Would you rather that I know all that without looking it up? Or that the Second World War started in 1939?"

Connor turned away from them and cringed. If his

father had witnessed that cheeky exchange, he would have been furious with him. But his father wasn't here, and the Mathers were still following him down the hall. Connor let himself feel a brief twinge of satisfaction as he approached a door where rainbow-colored letters announced, "Welcome, First Years!" Connor knocked on the door and then entered the classroom.

Inside were ten preschoolers lounging on beanbag chairs as they studied large, brightly-colored plastic models of the human heart. Miss Levine—who had been Connor's teacher back when he was a First Year—was kneeling next to a little girl.

As Connor and the Mathers approached, Miss Levine was asking the girl, "Emily, can you show me the coronary arteries?"

One at a time, Emily traced the arteries with her pointer finger. "Right coronary artery. Left coronary artery."

"What happens if they get blocked?" Miss Levine asked.

"Myocardial infarction," Emily said.

Miss Levine smiled. "Also called a heart attack. Very good." She affixed a smiley-face sticker to a page in a pocketsize pink notebook and handed the book to Emily.

Emily grinned and then turned her attention back to her plastic heart.

"How do they learn all that medical terminology?" Mr. Mather asked Miss Levine.

"The brain is set up to naturally acquire language until about age five," she explained. "Young children learn to understand and speak any language to which they are exposed. We expose our students to the language of medicine." She gestured to a row of plastic adult-sized chairs lined up against the back wall of the classroom. "Feel free to stay and observe as long as you like."

Miss Levine dismissed them with a nod and walked over to a keyboard, where she played a quick melody. Connor remembered the tune from his own preschool days. The children jumped up from their beanbags and stood at attention. Connor noticed that, even without meaning to, he was standing a little straighter as well.

"Time for heart sounds," Miss Levine announced cheerily.

Connor and the Mathers went to sit on the plastic

chairs and the preschoolers scurried to a shaggy, yellow circular rug in the center of the room. Once the children were seated, heart sounds—like the ones doctors hear through their stethoscopes—filled the air.

LUB SWISH. LUB SWISH. LUB SWISH. LUB SWISH—

Miss Levine paused the recording. "What's wrong with this patient's heart?" she asked the preschoolers.

Little hands shot up into the air.

Miss Levine selected a small boy to answer. "Jeremy?"

"VSD!" Jeremy shouted, as if he were addressing an army rather just the ten people gathered beside him.

"Ventricular septal defect, an abnormal hole between the pumping chambers of the heart. That's correct! Give me five," Miss Levine said. Jeremy high-fived her, and then Miss Levine continued, "Blood flow through the hole causes a harsh, holosystolic murmur like the one you just heard. Do small holes cause louder or softer murmurs than large holes?"

Hands shot into the air again. Miss Levine chose Emily to answer.

"Louder!" Emily said.

"No, softer!" Jeremy argued.

"I see we have a difference of opinion," Miss Levine said. "Let's figure out which answer is correct." She pulled a red balloon from a drawer, blew into the end until it was fully expanded, and then pinched it closed. "First, let's imagine a small VSD …" She unpinched the end of the balloon very slightly, and the balloon emitted a loud, high-pitched squeal.

Most of the children covered their ears. The others giggled.

"And now, a large VSD …" Miss Levine created a bigger opening in the end of the balloon. As the air escaped, it made a soft, low-pitched sound, like the sound of an old man passing gas out of his bottom.

The children erupted in laughter.

Miss Levine continued, "So, the smaller the VSD the …"

"… LOUDER …" the class said all together.

"… it sounds. Good!" Miss Levine said.

Mr. and Mrs. Mather looked at each other and smiled. Connor's gut told him that they were now strongly considering enrolling their daughter in the Kid Docs program. Connor had successfully done his job. But he didn't feel the delight that he normally felt when he eliminated prospective parents' doubts.

Maybe that was because he was starting to have doubts of his own.

* * *

"Oh good, you're back!" Hannah said to Connor when he arrived in the ER after returning the Mathers to his father's office. "Want to do some sewing?"

Connor was sure that Hannah was referring to sewing up a wound on a patient. "Suturing" was the technical term for it. Most ER doctors enjoy suturing—or doing almost any surgical procedure for that matter. It was strange that Hannah was inviting him to do her "fun" task for her.

Connor followed Hannah down the hallway. "Why don't *you* want to sew this one?"

"There's enough sewing to be done on this patient to occupy both of us," Hannah said, raising her eyebrows. "I'll sew one side. You can sew the other."

Connor braced himself for what he was about to see as Hannah pulled back a curtain. On the other side, Nurse Samantha was cleaning two gaping gashes in a burly man's legs—one wound in each thigh.

"How'd it happen?" Connor tried to sound nonchalant.

"Chainsaw," the patient said matter-of-factly.

Connor nodded and washed his hands. Then he opened a package of shiny, silver surgical instruments. The man eyed the pointy scissors and clamps as though they were devices that would be used to torture rather than heal him.

"Have you kids done this before?" the man asked, his voice raising an octave.

"Sir, I assure you that Doctor Connor and I are exceptionally competent at laceration repair," Hannah said. "Isn't that right, Doctor Connor?"

"Yes, indeed," Connor said. And it was true. They'd been suturing for years—first on artificial wounds, then on real patients.

"Okay, stay still now," Hannah instructed the patient.

Connor and Hannah pulled on sterile rubber gloves and injected numbing medicine into the man's wounds. Then they went to work, one doctor on each thigh. Connor carefully picked out small pieces of shredded clothing and he cut away bits of severely damaged skin and muscle to improve the chances that the wound would heal properly. As he worked, he frequently checked the man's face for signs of pain, but there were none. The numbing medicine had done its job. After a few minutes of watching them work, the man closed his eyes, his expression placid.

Once the wound was clean, Connor slid a threaded needle into one half of the man's meaty torn muscle. Then he pushed the needle though the opposite half and tied the thread, joining the two halves of the muscle back together again.

"How are you doing?" Connor asked his patient.

The man opened his eyes and smiled at him. "Doesn't hurt a bit. You kids are *good*!"

"Told ya!" Hannah said, grinning and doing a quick little dance. Even though she was starting to look like a teenager, Hannah still often acted like a little kid.

"Hey, are you guys brother and sister?" the man asked them.

Hannah and Connor weren't related, but when they were younger, people often mistook them for twins. They were almost the same age, had similarly thin builds, and their hair was exactly the same shade of blond. But over the past year, Hannah had grown a full two inches taller than Connor. Now people assumed she was his *older* sister. Connor hated it when people made that mistake. It made him feel even more like a child than he already did.

"No," Connor said before the man could say any more, and then he focused his attention back to his work.

He was almost finished closing the final layer of the man's skin when a loud, horrible sound came from the head of the bed. Startled, Connor looked at his patient, who let out another gurney-rattling, open-mouthed snore.

Hannah giggled. "We're so good that we put him to sleep!"

"Awesome," Connor said, smiling. But then, for some reason, his thoughts drifted to Mr. Peterson. His smile disappeared.

"What's wrong?" Hannah asked.

"Nothing."

Hannah pressed her lips together. She didn't seem to believe him, but rather than pushing any further she said, "My mom's making chicken tacos for dinner. Wanna come over?"

In spite of the unappetizing bloody gauze and

surgical instruments in front of him, Connor's mouth watered. Hannah's mom's chicken tacos were his favorite food in the world. But ... "I can't."

"Why not?" Hannah asked, eyes narrowed.

"I'm ... tired."

Connor hated lying, but he had plans for this evening that excited him even more than chicken tacos. Plans he couldn't tell Hannah anything about.

* * *

Connor muddled through the last hour of his shift. He determined that a fifteen-year-old boy with a sore throat needed antibiotics. He discovered that a sweet, elderly woman who'd had a cough for three weeks now had pneumonia. He closed a laceration on the forehead of a frightened five-year-old girl who calmed down quickly once Connor explained that he was going to use "magic glue"—instead of stitches—to help her cut get better. Then the night shift doctors arrived, and Connor was free to leave. His shift was over.

Connor's thoughts immediately turned to Mr. Peterson. He called the ICU and asked how his former patient was doing. Mr. Peterson's nurse told Connor that the surgeons had been able to repair the patient's torn spleen—which had been the source of the bleeding inside his belly—but that the ICU doctors were having trouble keeping Mr. Peterson's blood pressure stable.

When he hung up, Connor couldn't stop the guilt about Mr. Peterson from churning around in his stomach. He needed to talk to someone. Someone who would offer their honest thoughts. Someone he could trust, but who couldn't be disappointed in him because they were never proud of him.

His brother, Alex.

* * *

The hallway where the surgeons' private offices were located was quiet. Almost everyone had gone home for the day, but Connor was sure that Alex would still be there. For the past few years, even though his surgeries were scheduled to end by late afternoon, Alex stayed at the hospital until nine or ten at night. When Alex came home, he went straight to his room.

Up until a few years ago, Connor, Alex, and their dad ate dinner at home as a family nearly every evening. After dinner, they would sit in the living room and read or chat. But they didn't do that anymore. Nowadays, Connor and his dad would occasionally catch a quick dinner together—in the hospital cafeteria, because just the two of them eating at the family-sized dining room table at home was too sad. Most of the time though, Connor would grab something on his way home or eat with Hannah's family.

When Connor arrived at Alex's office, the door was closed, but Alex was inside. Connor heard him shouting, "You *always* say no. You didn't even ask where I wanted to go."

"Okay, where do you want to go?" a man responded. Connor recognized the voice. It was his dad's.

"Twenty Claws is going to be at Maren Stadium—"

"A *rock concert*? Absolutely not."

"Why not?" Alex sighed.

"The loud music can damage your hearing. And there's marijuana—"

"I'm not going to do drugs," Alex protested.

"It's in the air," his dad said. "And you're more likely to be kidnapped in crowded places."

"Isn't that why we wear those ridiculous tracking devices?" Alex was referring to the security bands that the Kid Docs wore around their ankles. Connor hated wearing his. It made him feel like a criminal.

"Those '*ridiculous* devices' are for your protection," his dad said.

"They're for *your* protection." Alex exhaled sharply. "Never mind. Forget it."

Connor realized that Alex wouldn't be in the mood to talk now, and Connor didn't want to be caught eavesdropping, so he started walking away, down the hallway. Behind him, he heard a door click open. Connor broke into a run for the nearest stairwell. He ducked inside and raced down the steps, all the way to the first floor, where he burst out and nearly ran into Cassie, again.

"Hey," Cassie said, looking amused.

Connor's skin flushed with embarrassment. He was sure that he must look silly, running out of the stairwell, breathless. "Let's get out of here," he said, quickly.

Cassie smiled. "Okay."

Chapter Two

Connor grabbed Cassie's arm, led her down the hallway, and pulled her into a different stairwell than the one he'd run down a few seconds before, then he released her and started up the stairs.

Cassie followed him. "Where are we going?" she asked, sounding a little nervous.

"To the top floor."

"Why aren't we taking the elevator?" she asked.

"The elevator doesn't go where we're going," Connor said.

"But ..." Cassie began, but then she seemed to reconsider.

They walked—without another word—to the very top of the stairwell, fifteen floors up, then Connor turned to Cassie. When he looked at her, he felt a strange, exhilarating tingling in his chest.

"Now what?" Cassie asked.

"It's kind of against the rules ..."

Cassie smiled in a way that made her face seem to glow and made Connor's face feel like it was hot and swollen. "All right."

"You're okay with breaking the rules?" Connor asked.

She shrugged. "I wasn't supposed to let you help deliver that baby today."

"But the nurse knows—"

"Nurse Sandra is cool. She doesn't care what I do as long as it doesn't interfere with the patients' care."

Cassie's relationship with Nurse Sandra sounded a lot like Connor's relationship with Nurse Samantha and Nurse Mike. But Connor hadn't told either of them *this* secret.

"You can't tell *anyone* about this," Connor said firmly.

"I won't. I promise." She stared into Connor's eyes in a way that made him uncomfortable and excited at the same time. "So what are we going to do?"

"Go up that." Connor pointed to a narrow metal ladder leading to a hatch in the ceiling, about fifteen feet above them.

Cassie's eyes widened as if he'd just suggested that they leap off a skyscraper. "No way!"

Connor exhaled, disappointment chilling his

excitement. "Why not?"

She shook her head. "It's too dangerous."

"Not really," Connor said. "I've done it loads of times."

Her forehead furrowed. "Why?"

Through the hatch was the hospital roof. He remembered the many times he stood on the rooftop, looking out at the world, wind caressing his face. He smiled. "Because from the roof … you can see forever."

Cassie glanced from Connor to the ladder and back again, her lips pressed tightly together. Finally, she said, "Okay. But you go first."

Connor could barely suppress the thrill of anticipation. He grabbed hold of the ladder and started up. He was halfway to the hatch when Cassie began climbing below him, breathing slowly and deliberately.

"You okay down there?" Connor whispered to her. He didn't want his voice to echo too much in the stairwell.

"I let you deliver a baby and this is how you repay me?" Cassie asked, moving up the ladder very slowly.

"I didn't exactly *want* to delivery a baby," Connor

said.

"Oh," Cassie said, a bit of hurt in her voice.

"But … I'm glad I did it, because even though it was fairly gross, it was really cool," Connor added as he arrived at the top of the ladder. He grabbed the combination lock on the hatch and pulled, but the lock held tight.

"It's locked." Cassie started back down the ladder.

"Not for long. I treated one of the custodians in the ER. After we fixed him up, he was so grateful that he gave me the combination." Connor opened the lock, pushed up the hatch, and climbed through.

Cassie inhaled deeply and climbed to the top of the ladder. She crawled onto the roof on all fours, gave a quick glance around, and said, "Okay, I've seen it. Let's go down."

"You haven't seen anything." Connor hopped to his feet and headed around the side of a metal structure about the size of a tool shed.

Cassie shook her head and followed him. When she rounded the corner, Connor was climbing a skinny, rusted ladder. It was similar in height to the one they'd just climbed, but its location—right near the edge of the roof—made climbing this one seem much more intimidating.

"Come on," Connor called to her.

Cassie stared at the ladder. "What if I fall?"

"How many slippery little babies have you delivered?"

"Over a thousand."

"Ever dropped one?"

"No."

"Then you're not gonna fall."

Cassie grabbed hold of the ladder, looking determined, and started to climb. But the higher she climbed, the more slowly she moved. When she was just five rungs from the top, Cassie stopped, frozen in place. "I'm too scared, Connor," she murmured, her voice shaking.

"Concentrate on climbing the ladder. Don't think about anything else."

Cassie didn't move.

"Left foot," Connor said, unsure whether she'd follow his instructions.

After a moment, Cassie moved her left foot up to the next rung.

"Good job," Connor said. "Left hand."

Cassie moved her left hand up a rung.

Connor coached, and Cassie climbed—one extremity at a time—until she reached the top. She crawled into Connor's arms, her body shivering even though the air wasn't very cold and the breeze was gentle.

And then she exclaimed, "Oh wow!"

"What?" Connor asked, pulling away.

Cassie gazed at the sky, her lips parted in awe. The setting sun had filled it with a magical display of colors that bounced off the reflective windows of the office buildings surrounding the hospital. "You *can* see forever," she said.

Cassie settled next to him, her arm just barely touching his. Her trembling lessened and her breathing slowed as they watched the evening turn to night.

* * *

Nurse Samantha poked her head into the ER doctors' room. "Doctor Connor, we need you in Trauma One!"

Connor jumped up from his seat and rushed down the hallway, toward Trauma Room One. Inside, Nurse Mike was covering a man's body with large blue surgical drapes, leaving only the patient's chest exposed. The heart monitor attached to the patient showed a flat line. The man's heart had stopped.

Mario—a tall, thin, raven-haired ER doctor who was one year older than Connor—was in charge. "Resume CPR," he barked.

A medical student started pushing on the patient's chest, pumping the man's heart.

Mario spotted Connor. "Ready to do your first emergency thoracotomy?"

An emergency thoracotomy is a procedure that ER doctors rarely perform. It is a last ditch effort to try to save someone's life. Doing an emergency thoracotomy involves quickly cutting open the patient's ribcage and searching the chest for a problem that can be rapidly fixed. Unfortunately, most of the time, the problem that is found is too severe to repair fast enough to save the patient.

Even though he had been thoroughly trained in how to perform a thoracotomy, Connor didn't feel ready for this, but he said what he'd been taught to say, "I need a thoracotomy tray and size six and a half sterile gloves."

A tray was moved into position by Connor's side. As Connor pulled on a sterile gown and gloves, Mario told Connor about what had happened to the patient.

The man had been in a car accident. An ultrasound had shown that there was fluid filling the man's chest. Mario had put a tube into the chest to drain out the fluid and a whole lot of blood had poured out. They needed to find out where the bleeding was coming from and stop it.

Connor lifted a scalpel from the tray. He sliced through the skin and muscles between the patient's ribs, creating a long, deep gash from the center of the man's chest to his armpit.

"Hold ventilations," Connor told Hannah—who had been periodically squeezing a resuscitation bag attached to a breathing tube running into the patient's mouth.

"Holding ventilations," Hannah said, and she immediately stopped squeezing the bag.

Connor pierced the man's chest cavity with his scalpel. There was a tiny pop as some air escaped.

"Resume ventilations," Connor ordered.

He grabbed some scissors and cut through the final layer of tissue. Now, the man's chest was completely cut open. The wound gaped. Connor slid a metal rib spreader between the ribs and cranked the jaws apart, so that he had a larger opening from which to explore. He could hear the man's bones crack as the ribs were pushed apart.

Blood poured out from the patient's chest, wetting the surgical drapes and spilling onto the trauma room floor.

"Suction," Connor shouted.

Nurse Samantha used a clear hollow tube attached to a thin hose to suck up the blood pooling inside the man's chest, but more blood instantly took its place, faster than she could suction it up. Connor moved the man's pink, spongy lungs out of the way and lifted something from the lake of blood: the man's lifeless heart. Blood oozed from a tiny tear in the heart muscle. Connor covered the tear with his finger.

"Stapler!" Connor called out.

A wound stapler was dropped onto Connor's tray.

As Connor stapled the heart wound closed, Nurse Samantha suctioned away the remaining blood in the man's chest cavity. It was easy now that Connor had stopped the blood from pouring out of the patient's injured heart.

Once Connor was done repairing the heart, he flicked it with his finger—the way he'd once seen Alex do in the operating room. The heart immediately started beating again. Connor felt like a hero. Against the odds, the thoracotomy had saved his patient's life.

But then, without warning, blood once again began to fill the man's chest. Connor checked the heart. It seemed fine. His repair was holding and the heart was pumping. But it wouldn't be pumping for long, not when the man was losing this much blood.

Connor frantically searched for the source of the bleeding. "I missed something," Connor said under his breath.

He moved the lungs out of the way, but they flopped back, blocking his view. Nurse Samantha tried to suction away the blood, but it was coming even faster than before.

"It's my fault!" Connor screamed. "It's my fault!"

And then, he woke up, sweaty and shaky, his heart pounding as if he'd just run a marathon.

Usually when Connor woke up from a nightmare, he felt relieved that it was only a dream, but this time, waking up didn't make him feel any better.

All he could think about was Mr. Peterson.

* * *

Still wearing his pajamas, Connor trudged out of his

bedroom, through the dark hallway, down the stairs, through the living room, and out the front door of his house.

His house was one of many nearly-identical houses on the quiet, well-manicured, tree-lined streets in the gated community behind Westley Hospital. Inside the other houses were the other Kid Docs' families.

Under the glow of the street lights, he walked up one block, to a park where there was a huge deserted playground complete with almost every type of playground equipment imaginable. Connor had been playing on that playground ever since he was a little kid. He secretly wished he still could play there, even though he knew he was much too old to be seen playing on a playground.

Connor leaned his back against the jungle gym and lowered himself to the squishy mats beneath it, his bottom hitting the ground with a dull thud. Just then, he saw a shadow moving toward him. A street light illuminated the shadow's face. It was Alex.

It was almost midnight. It was strange for Alex to be getting home this late, unless there was an emergency surgery.

Alex spotted him and his brow creased. "Connor, what are you doing out here?"

"I can't sleep," Connor said, and then he asked, "Was there an emergency at the hospital?"

"No, I had some ... paperwork to finish," Alex said. Connor could tell by the way he said it, that it his brother's explanation wasn't the truth. Connor wondered what Alex was *really* doing out so late. Alex seemed to sense Connor's suspicion. Alex's gaze shifted away from him. "Why can't you sleep?"

"Bad dream."

"About what?"

Connor took a deep breath. He'd wanted to talk to someone about this all day, and Alex was the only person he felt he could tell. "There was a patient who came into the ER today after a car accident. He was in cardiac arrest. We got him back—"

"That's great."

"But it was my fault that he needed saving."

Alex frowned. "What?"

"I treated the same man in the ER yesterday too. I was his doctor and I messed up."

Alex sat on the bottom of the slide. "What happened?"

"Yesterday, he came into the ER with a chief complaint of chest pain. I sent him home. Then, today, he got in a car crash. When the paramedics found him, he was in v-fib. He probably had a heart attack while he was driving. I never should have sent him home."

"Did you check his heart yesterday?"

"Yeah. All of his tests were normal."

Alex exhaled. "Then I think most doctors would have sent him home. Exactly like you did."

"But I don't want to be like 'most doctors.' I want to be one of the best," Connor said.

"Well, that's why we're here, isn't it?" Alex said, staring at the ground.

Alex was an amazing doctor. He was world-renowned. But, strangely, he didn't seem happy.

"Alex, do you like being a doctor?" Connor asked.

"Sure," he said, rising to his feet. "Let's go home. It's late."

By the time Connor stood up, Alex was already nearly a quarter of a block ahead of him. Connor caught up with his brother, and then he walked silently by Alex's side the rest of the way.

Chapter Three

The next day, during his lunch break, Connor took the elevator from the ER to the third floor. He scanned his doctor badge at the entrance to the labor and delivery unit, and then walked down the noisy corridor, listening to the same characteristic cries of pain that he'd heard from women in the ER who were delivering their babies—but here there were a chorus of them. He glanced into room after room until he found who he was looking for.

Cassie was sewing up a wound on a sleeping patient. Nurse Sandra typed on a computer nearby. Another nurse tended to the newborn baby.

"Can I help you?" the baby's nurse asked Connor.

Cassie looked up from her work. When she saw Connor standing in the doorway, her eyes widened with trepidation. "Connor, what are you doing here?"

Connor felt all of the eyes in the room on him. "I … just came to … check on the patient you saw in the emergency room yesterday."

Cassie exhaled. "Mother and baby are doing very

well."

"Good!" Connor declared. "Oh ... and I was reading up on shoulder dystocia and I had some questions for you." Connor wasn't exactly sure what shoulder dystocia was, but he remembered an obstetrician mentioning the term in the ER once.

"We could discuss your questions after work," Cassie suggested.

"That would be ... great. Why don't you come by my office at five-thirty?"

"Your office?" Cassie asked. Only the senior doctors had offices. The junior doctors just had group lounges where they could sit and relax during their break times.

"You know, *upstairs*," Connor said.

Cassie nodded, her brow creased. "Oh, okay. I'll see you there at five-thirty."

"Cool," Connor said, trying to sound nonchalant. "I look forward to it." With that, Connor exited the room, his face burning with embarrassment at the awkward way he'd handled that conversation.

As he stepped into the hallway, Connor heard one of the nurses quietly ask Cassie, "Is that your boyfriend?"

Connor stopped in his tracks and listened for Cassie's response, but just then, an IV pump started beeping to indicate that it needed to be checked. Connor couldn't hear what Cassie said or whether she said anything at all.

* * *

Connor made sure to finish his work on time that day, and he arrived on the roof of the hospital about twenty minutes before five thirty. Moments later, he heard a light knock from the hatch. He dashed over and opened it, and Cassie emerged.

"Hey!" Her voice was a little shaky.

Connor offered her his hand. "Hey!"

Cassie took hold of Connor's hand, letting him help her up onto the roof, but once she was safely there, she didn't let go.

Connor looked down at their clasped hands, feeling tingly all through his chest. He gestured to the walkway around the edge of the roof. "Would you … like to go for a walk?"

Cassie eyed the narrow walkway, separated by a thin railing from a steep drop. Her forehead creased, but she said, "Okay."

As they turned the first corner, Cassie said, "Nurse Sandra thinks you're my boyfriend."

"Why?" Connor asked, even though he had a pretty good idea why.

Cassie looked away from him. "I don't know."

"*Am* I your boyfriend?" Connor asked.

Cassie shrugged.

Connor had never had a girlfriend before. He had never really wanted one. But Cassie was special, and she made him feel special too. He felt like she understood him in a way that no one ever had before. He was excited to be close to her, even though staring into her eyes terrified him. She seemed to feel the same way about him.

"I think I *am* your boyfriend," Connor said softly.

"No, you're not," Cassie countered.

But they were still holding hands.

Connor was confused. Maybe he was wrong about Cassie's feelings. "We don't have to hold hands if you don't want to." He loosened his grip, but instead of taking that as an invitation to let go, Cassie held his hand even more tightly.

Cassie stared into his eyes. "Don't let go."

Connor wasn't sure whether she was holding his

hand out of fear or something else. He took a deep breath and stared back at her. "Okay," he said, his voice barely a whisper.

And then Cassie's foot slipped. And she slid, feet first, along the steep metal roof, heading toward the edge, dragging Connor with her by their still-clasped hands. Connor instinctively grabbed hold of the walkway railing with his free hand, but the railing broke loose, traveling with them until it caught on one final bolt.

They stopped moving—fifteen stories above the unforgiving street below.

Cassie looked down in horror. "Connor, help me!"

"Hold on. I'll pull you up." Connor tried to pull Cassie toward him, but she hardly budged. The railing in his other hand gave a little. Dizzying fear tickled through him.

"My leg's caught," Cassie said.

Connor looked down. A metal wire was wrapped around Cassie's security ankle bracelet. Cassie struggled to free herself, but the wire just dug deeper into her leg. She cringed in pain.

Connor knew what he had to do. It was dangerous, but he didn't see any other viable option.

"See if you can get hold of the railing," he said. The far end of the broken railing looked close enough to Cassie that she might be able to grab onto it.

"Why?" Cassie said, her voice shaky.

"I'm going to climb down and get your foot loose," Connor said.

Cassie stared at him, terror in her eyes. "You're going to let go?"

"I won't let go of you until you grab the railing. I promise."

Cassie looked at him, tears forming in her eyes. "But what will *you* hold onto."

Connor didn't say the answer. Because the answer was *nothing*. "I'll be fine," he said instead. "Go ahead and grab the railing."

Cassie stretched her free hand toward the broken railing, but she could barely touch the closest portion with the tips of her trembling fingers. "I can't reach it," she said.

Connor's stomach sank. He was going to have to pull the railing closer to Cassie. But if he pulled it too far, the bolt could give, sending the railing—and the two of them—over the edge.

His heart pounding in his throat, Connor carefully

rotated the railing, keeping his eye on the one little bolt. As he turned it, to Connor's horror, the metal railing began to tear. Connor stopped immediately. He didn't dare rotate it anymore. He hoped what he'd done was enough.

"Try now," he said to Cassie.

Cassie reached up and wrapped her fingertips around the railing. "I've got it, sort of."

Cassie didn't have a very good grip on the railing, but it would have to do.

"Good," Connor said to her. "I'm going to let go of your hand now."

Cassie nodded and closed her eyes.

"You let go first," he said.

Slowly, Cassie released her grip. Connor gradually released his too, until their hands had fully separated. He gave one final glance at Cassie's tenuous grip on the railing and began slinking down the roof, his sweaty palms and the rubbery soles of his sneakers pressed against the hot metal.

Connor inched his way toward Cassie's tethered foot. Her white sock was wet with blood. Dark blood oozed from the gash where the wire was impaled in her leg.

"Is it bleeding bad?" Cassie asked.

"It's okay. It doesn't look arterial."

"Connor?" Cassie said weakly. "Are *you* okay?"

"Yeah, I'm good." But there was a lot to accomplish before he and Cassie were safe.

Connor pulled out his ER trauma scissors and used them to gnaw his way through the thick wire tangled around Cassie's ankle band. He knew better than to bother trying to cut her ankle band. Those security bands couldn't be cut.

When he made his final snip through the wire, the bit that had been stuck in Cassie's leg flew out and disappeared over the edge. Connor shivered at the reminder of the danger just inches away from him. He scrambled up to the walkway on all fours, thinking about how he used to climb up the slide at the playground as a kid whenever there were no adults around to scold him for doing so. He never thought his playground skills would help save his life.

As soon as he was on the walkway, he put his belly flat on the ground and extended his arms toward Cassie. She looked into Connor's eyes, seeming to draw strength from them. Then she grabbed hold of his hands, first one, then the other.

Connor used every ounce of his strength—more than he thought he had—to pull Cassie up to safety. Once they were both securely on the walkway, they sat next to each other, not talking. Connor tried to hide the shaking in his muscles from the adrenaline still coursing through him. He finally gave up, because Cassie was shaking too.

After a few minutes, Cassie lifted the leg of her scrub pants and examined her wound.

"I'm sorry, Cassie," Connor said.

"I've seen worse," she said, as if she were trying to reassure him. And then she gave him a half smile. "So, are you gonna sew me up?"

* * *

Cassie sat semi-reclined on an ER gurney. Her right lower leg was mostly covered by blue drape sheets. Only the wound on her leg was left exposed.

Connor slid a tiny curved needle into Cassie's skin, through her wound, and out the other side. Fortunately for Cassie, the medicine Connor had used to numb up her wound had worked so well that she didn't feel any pain at all. Unfortunately for Connor, Cassie was watching him work so closely that she was making him self-conscious.

"Do you have to watch me like that?" Connor asked her.

"Why?" Cassie responded. "Am I making you nervous?"

"No," Connor lied.

"Good," Cassie said. "You know, your stitches are very nice. Symmetrical. Evenly spaced—"

"Thank you," Connor cut her off, even though she was complimenting him.

Cassie sighed and leaned back on the gurney, much to Connor's relief. He finished sewing in silence. Once Cassie was no longer staring at him, he was able to sew much faster.

"That should so it," Connor said, as he covered the wound with a bandage.

"Thanks," Cassie said.

As Cassie pulled the blue drapes from her leg and adjusted her scrub pants, Connor noticed, "You've got a lot of bruises." There were at least seven that he could see, and they were old bruises, not from today's events.

"I bruise easily," she said, and then she admitted, "Maybe a little more easily lately."

Connor was certain that Cassie knew this wasn't normal. Connor had seen bruising like hers twice before, on two different patients. Both of those patients had cancer.

"Have you been having fevers?" he asked.

"Ninety-nines," Cassie said quietly. "For over a week," she added.

Connor's heart pounded with concern. "You need to have a doctor check you out," he said.

"Could *you* check me?"

Connor shook his head. "That's not a good idea." The thought of examining Cassie as if she were a patient scared him, mostly because he was afraid that he might find evidence of a serious problem.

"You're a doctor," she said.

"Yes, but I'm also your ..." Connor wasn't sure what to say next. Finally, he decided to say, "friend," but he was fairly certain that they were more than just friends.

Cassie looked into his eyes. "Please, Connor."

Connor knew deep in his heart that, if the situation were reversed, Cassie would help him. And so, even though it made his gut twist with unease, Connor grabbed a stethoscope and listened to Cassie's heart.

Her heart was beating faster than normal, probably because she was anxious. He listened to her lungs as she took slow deep breaths.

So far he'd found nothing concerning, but that was about to change. When Connor felt the sides of Cassie's neck, he discovered numerous firm lumps. Her lymph nodes were swollen. When he pressed on Cassie's belly, he felt a mass on the upper left side and another one on the right side. Cassie's liver and spleen were enlarged.

"Do you have any known medical problems?" Connor asked.

"No."

"Taking any medications?"

"No."

"I need to run some tests." Connor started off to go get some blood drawing supplies.

"How was the exam?" Cassie asked, her voice unsteady.

Connor turned back to her and said gently, "You're mildly tachycardiac, and you have lymphadenopathy and hepatosplenomegally."

She pressed her lips together, and then she asked, "This could be cancer ... leukemia?"

"There are other possibilities," Connor said.

"But cancer is one of them," she said. "A big one."

"Yes," he said, and then he turned away and rushed out the door.

Connor hated himself for not comforting her, but there was no comfort to be had here. The only comfort would come by running tests that proved Cassie didn't have a serious diagnosis. But those same tests could also confirm her worst fears. There was a very strong possibility that Cassie, his friend—maybe even his girlfriend—was extremely sick. And if she was, there would be nothing Connor could say or do to fix that.

Chapter Four

As Connor entered the ER hallway, he heard someone call his name. He turned and saw Hannah.

"Hey, Hannah," Connor said, trying to act casual.

"Hi," Hannah replied. "What are you still doing here? Your shift was over two hours ago."

"I'm doing a favor for a friend." Without meaning to, Connor glanced back toward the room he'd just exited.

Hannah looked into the room and saw Cassie lying on the gurney. "Is she a doctor here?"

"Yeah," Connor said, wishing the conversation was over. He tried to change the subject. "What are *you* still doing here?"

"I followed one of my patients up to the OR to observe their surgery," Hannah answered, but she stayed focused on Cassie. "What year is she?"

Connor and Hannah were Eleventh Years. Connor didn't know what year Cassie was. It felt to Connor like Cassie was the same age as him, but she couldn't be. He knew all of the other Eleventh Years. They had gone to preschool together and then, even though they separated to learn their specialties, they still got together from time to time. And Cassie couldn't be a year below him because Kid Docs weren't allowed to work independently in the hospital until they were Eleventh Years.

And so Connor answered, "I guess she's a Twelfth Year."

"Your girlfriend is an *older woman*?" Hannah teased.

"She's not my girlfriend. We're just friends," Connor said.

"Are you sure?" Hannah asked, her eyes narrowed.

"I think I would know if she's my girlfriend." But the fact was, he didn't.

"So what kind of favor are you doing for her?" Hannah asked.

Connor knew that, if he refused to answer, Hannah wouldn't leave him alone, and so he said, "I sewed up a cut for her."

"We're not allowed to treat each other without supervision," Hannah said.

Hannah was a stickler when it came to rules.

Ordinarily, Connor respected her for that, but right now, he wished she would just relax about the rules a little.

"We're not little medical students anymore," Connor said. "Sewing up a cut is no big deal. I don't think I need a grown-up doctor looking over my shoulder when I do that. Plus it was kind of my fault she got the cut in the first place."

"You *cut* her?"

Connor couldn't tell Hannah that he and Cassie had gone up to the hospital roof. That was against the rules too. Connor had never taken Hannah up to the roof or even told her about his frequent trips to the roof for that very reason. He thought for a second before he answered truthfully, "I invited her on a walk, and she slipped and fell."

Amazingly, Hannah accepted his explanation. "Oh."

"I've gotta go," Connor said, breaking away from her. "I'll see you tomorrow."

"Yeah," Hannah said. And then—strangely—she turned and walked back the same way she'd come.

In an empty trauma room, Connor slipped some blood drawing supplies into his pocket. Then he went back to Cassie.

"Come on," Connor said to her. "We need to do this somewhere else." He couldn't draw her blood in the ER anymore, just in case Hannah came back.

Cassie didn't ask any questions. She jumped down from the gurney and followed him.

* * *

"We can use my brother's office," Connor said to Cassie as the elevator doors opened on the fourteenth floor. "Alex said he was going to hang out with his friends after work today."

"He lets you use his office?" she asked.

"He doesn't know. I figured out the security code. Alex is super-predictable sometimes."

Connor knocked on Alex's door, just to make sure he wasn't inside, and then dialed in the combination—the birth date of Twenty Claws' lead singer. The door popped open, and Cassie and Connor stepped inside the office.

But it wasn't empty. Alex was sitting on the floor with five of his friends—four guys and one girl. Connor felt as if the air in the room had become too thick to breathe.

"Connor," Alex growled, his eyes wide with fury, "how'd you get in here?"

But Connor didn't answer. He was staring at Alex, shocked by what he saw. Alex's pants leg was pulled up, and he was holding a dangerous-looking device that had sharp blades at one end and the word "OSTEOCISOR" printed in bold letters along one of the handles. On the floor was Alex's security ankle band. *It had been cut off.*

Up until that moment, Connor had thought it was impossible for the security bands to be cut. That's what he'd been told ever since he was a little kid. Just to be certain, a few of Connor's friends had tried cutting through the bands using ER trauma scissors and various other cutting devices, but nothing made even a scratch on the security bands.

It bothered him to see Alex's security band lying on the floor. For as long as he could remember, those bands had been part of their lives. Connor didn't like the bands, but he could always count on them being there, no matter what. Now, suddenly, Alex's wasn't.

"Why did you cut off your band?" he whispered at Alex.

"You can't tell anybody about this. You

understand?" Alex said roughly.

Connor and Cassie shook their heads in reluctant agreement.

"But why did you cut it off?" Connor asked again.

"There's something I need to go do," Alex answered.

Chris—one of Alex's friends—piped up, "Why don't we bring your brother along?"

"Bring me where?" Connor asked, his curiosity tempered by apprehension.

Alex thought for a moment and then said, "Twenty Claws having a concert at Maren Stadium tomorrow night. We're going, and you're coming with us."

Connor had absolutely no interest in going to a Twenty Claws concert. Their music made his head ache. But hanging out with his brother for a few hours could be fun, like when they were younger and Alex actually enjoyed being around him.

"Okay … Thanks," Connor said.

"Your girlfriend is coming too," Alex added, looking at Cassie.

Connor looked at Cassie who smiled uncomfortably.

"All right," Alex said to the group, "we'll meet here at six tomorrow night, I'll cut off everyone's security bands, and then we'll go see Twenty Claws!"

Alex's friends let out a great big whoop in response, pumping their fists in the air.

Alex glared at Connor and Cassie, who were sitting quietly, and they quickly mustered a small self-conscious whoop, awkwardly raising their fists like Alex's friends had done.

"Meeting adjourned," Alex said.

Alex's friends quietly funneled out of the office.

Alex patted Connor on the shoulder, almost tenderly. "See ya at home."

Connor and Cassie walked into the hallway, and Alex gently closed his door behind them.

It was late, but Connor couldn't head home yet, he still had to draw Cassie's blood. He searched his brain, trying to think of somewhere they could go where no one would see them.

Then he remembered the perfect place.

* * *

Connor and Cassie entered an uninhabited hospital ward. Dim orange emergency lights provided the only illumination. This was once the place where the sickest children in Westley Hospital were taken care of: the pediatric intensive care unit, or PICU for short. When the hospital got a big donation and built a brand new PICU, they closed this one. The administrators planned to eventually turn the old PICU into something else, but they hadn't figured out what yet, so it remained empty, silent, and creepy.

"The only people who will see us here are ghosts," Connor said.

"Ghosts?" Cassie asked, looking around anxiously.

"I'm just kidding. My brother and I used to play in here and pretend there were ghosts, but there aren't," Connor reassured her. He felt a stab of sadness in his belly, remembering nights spent running through the old PICU with his brother, shrieking with laughter as they hid and scared each other.

In the center of the main room was a long, curved nurses' station desk. Branching off the room were twenty smaller rooms with large glass windows. The wallpaper inside the rooms—decorated with cartoon characters—was starting to peel and fade. The beds, medical equipment, and even the chairs had been removed.

Connor led Cassie to the nurses' station desk. "Have a seat."

Cassie sat on the desk, because there was no other choice for a place to sit. Connor assembled his supplies and tied a rubber tourniquet band around Cassie's upper arm. Then he lightly poked at her inner elbow with the tip of his pointer finger, searching for a plump, spongy vein.

"Are you good at drawing blood?" Cassie asked, although it seemed a little late to ask that question.

"I don't do it a lot. Usually the nurses draw our patients' blood," Connor said. "But I'm excellent at art lines."

"Don't you dare put anything in any of my arteries," Cassie said, pulling away her arm.

"Don't worry," Connor said. "I'll avoid your arteries."

"Thank you," Cassie said, letting him take hold of her arm again.

Connor swabbed a small area of her arm with a tiny pad soaked in alcohol and uncapped a needle. Cassie looked away as the needle approached her arm.

"Little pinch," Connor warned, then he darted the

needle into Cassie's skin.

A flash of blood instantly appeared in the tubing, indicating that the needle had successfully entered Cassie's vein. Connor slid a blood collection tube onto a small cup at the end of the tubing, and Cassie's blood rushed into the tube. Connor felt a weird lightness in his head from seeing Cassie's blood like that. He shook off the feeling and pulled off the full tube.

He was about to fill another tube when Cassie's upper body abruptly fell onto him, as if she had suddenly lost all muscle tone. Her face was pale, but she was breathing.

Connor released the tourniquet from Cassie's arm, pulled out the needle, and pressed a folded piece of gauze against Cassie's skin. If Cassie platelets were low—and they probably were—her blood wouldn't clot very well. She could end up with a huge bruise, or worse.

Connor carefully eased Cassie onto the desk. He stared at her ashen face, watching her chest rise and fall with each breath, his fingers sensing the faint, but steady pulse in her wrist.

After a few moments, Cassie opened her eyes

slightly, appearing as if she was having trouble making her eyes focus on anything. "I passed out," she murmured as she started to get up.

"Don't get up. Just rest." Connor stretched out next to her, hoping that would encourage her to stay put.

"Why did I pass out?" Cassie said. "I see blood all the time, and it doesn't bother me."

"It's different when it's your own," Connor said.

Cassie shrugged. "I guess."

"If it makes you feel any better, it was weird for me … seeing your blood." Connor felt his face burn. That thought had sounded much better in his head than it did coming out of his mouth.

Cassie looked at him, finally appearing to be able to focus. "That doesn't make me feel any better. But that's really sweet." She rolled onto her side so they were face-to-face. "You're really sweet, Connor."

And then there was a loud *CRASH*.

Cassie and Connor bolted upright.

"What was that?" Cassie asked.

"Maybe something fell."

"Or was pushed … by a ghost."

"Let's get out of here." Connor snatched the tube

of Cassie's blood from the desk, grabbed Cassie's hand, and—leaving everything else behind—tore out of the PICU, wondering whether it might *actually* be haunted.

Chapter Five

Connor opened the front door to his house as quietly as he could. If his dad heard him come in, he would ask why he was getting home so late. Connor didn't want to lie to him, but he couldn't tell him the truth. He hoped his dad had gone to sleep early.

When he stepped into the living room, he knew immediately that wasn't the case.

"What's your excuse?" his dad practically yelled. But he wasn't speaking to Connor.

"I was mad, okay?" Alex sighed.

Connor snuck, unnoticed, into the bathroom by the front door.

"No, it's not okay," his dad said. "You threw surgical instruments on the floor *during a surgery*."

Connor's mouth dropped open. He couldn't believe Alex had done that.

"The surgery was almost over," Alex retorted.

His dad exhaled. "Alex—"

"The stupid scissors didn't work. Maybe you should look into that."

"I don't think this is about the scissors."

"Maybe it's about *you*."

They were silent for a moment. And then his dad said—so softly that Connor barely heard him, "Maybe it is."

"You never let me do anything. I'm sixteen years old. I should be able to make decisions for myself."

"Other sixteen-year-olds don't get to decide everything for themselves."

"But I'm a doctor. I'm more mature than other sixteen-year-olds."

"You didn't act very mature in the OR today."

"Adult surgeons throw things sometimes too. I've seen them." Alex always had an answer for everything. That was part of what made him such a great surgeon, but it also made him really hard to argue with. His dad often said that, if Alex hadn't become a doctor, he would have probably become a lawyer.

"I can see we're not getting anywhere," his dad said.

"So that's it?" Alex asked.

"No, that's not it. You're grounded, and you're on probation. I've rescheduled all of your surgeries for tomorrow so you can reflect on what you did and on the harm that could have come to the patient and the OR team. Starting Monday, all of your cases will be proctored by an adult surgeon for one month. If there are no further incidents, you will be removed from proctoring."

"What if there *are* further incidents?" Alex asked angrily. "Will I be expelled?"

"You will be punished."

"What if I don't want to be a doctor anymore?" It sounded more like a threat than a question.

"Don't be ridiculous, Alex. You are a gifted surgeon."

"I wish I had parents. If I did, I'd be so out of here. Instead, all I have is you. And you *suck*!"

Connor heard Alex's feet pounding up the stairs, and then an upstairs door slammed shut. A few moments later, he heard his dad's footsteps heading up the stairs, then another upstairs door closed. Connor sat on the lid of the toilet and waited a few minutes. Hearing nothing further, he slunk upstairs to his bedroom. He inched his bedroom door open and then closed.

Just then, his pager beeped loudly. Initially,

Connor was relieved that it hadn't gone off a few minutes earlier, but when he checked the number, his entire body tensed.

The hospital laboratory had paged him. They were calling with the results of Cassie's blood tests.

Connor grabbed his phone and dialed. A woman answered.

"This is Doctor Connor. I was paged," Connor said to her.

"Yes, Doctor Connor," she said, her tone urgent, "I have some critical values on your patient, Jane Doe, medical record number: 4752388."

Jane Doe is a temporary name that doctors and nurses use for patients at the hospital whom no one can identify. Connor had used the Jane Doe name instead of Cassie's real name so no one would know that Cassie was sick.

"Go ahead," Connor said, sitting down on the edge of his bed.

"There are a lot of abnormal values," she said. "Where would you like me to start?"

"What's her platelet count?" Connor asked.

"Thirty-four thousand," she answered.

Cassie's platelets were low. That explained her

bruising.

"How about her white blood cell count?"

"Three point six," the woman responded.

That was also low. Connor's pulse pounded in his neck.

"Is she anemic?" he asked, hoping she wasn't.

"Yes. Hemoglobin's ten point one."

Connor swallowed his dread. "Can you send the rest of the results to my phone?" he asked, fighting to keep his tone professional.

"Done," she said.

"Thank you." Connor ended the call, opened Cassie's lab report, and scrolled through the results. Seeing all those abnormal numbers on the screen and knowing what they meant for Cassie, Connor felt like he might throw up. But he closed his eyes for a moment, took a deep breath, and then did what he would do for any other patient: he called Westley Hospital's best blood disorder and cancer doctor, Doctor Keith. Doctor Keith was two years ahead of Connor. Connor told him about Cassie's symptoms, exam, and lab results and asked for his recommendations on what to do next. He didn't tell Doctor Keith that Cassie was a Kid Doc.

Doctor Keith gave Connor a list of additional blood tests to perform on Cassie to try to determine a diagnosis.

Then Connor asked him, "Do you think I need to call the patient back to the hospital tonight, or is it okay to wait until morning?"

"Let the family sleep. They're going to need it. Call them in the morning."

"Okay," Connor said. "Thanks for your help."

"Good night," Doctor Keith said.

"Good night."

But it wouldn't be a good night. Not for Connor.

* * *

Connor had a restless night's sleep that he was sure was filled with nightmares—though he didn't remember any of them. He dragged himself out of bed and sent Cassie a text message:

Meet me at Alex's office at 7AM.

Even when Alex wasn't grounded, he was never in his office before ten in the morning. Alex stayed up late and slept in. He would sleep until noon every day if his dad let him. On his days off, Alex did.

Cassie must have been awake when she got Connor's text because, an instant after he sent it, she texted back:

OK

Connor washed up and threw on his doctor scrubs. He skipped breakfast—because, even though he hadn't eaten dinner, he wasn't the least bit hungry—and went to the hospital.

He arrived at Alex's office ten minutes before seven. He went inside and sat down at Alex's desk. When he was younger, Connor used to enjoy sitting there, imagining what it was like to be in Alex's shoes. Alex had a perfect life. He was successful and respected. *How could Alex be so unhappy?*

There was a soft knock at the door.

"Come in," Connor said.

Cassie entered and looked at Connor for a moment before she sat down stiffly on the couch across from Alex's desk. The skin under her eyes was puffy and dark. She didn't look like she had slept much last night. Connor walked out from behind

Alex's desk and sat next to her.

"Well?" Cassie asked, her voice weak.

"Your bruising is due to a decreased platelet count. Your white count and hemoglobin are also low. I spoke with Doctor Keith. He's our best hematologist/oncologist—"

"I have cancer?"

"Doctor Keith suggested a few more tests."

Cassie shook her head. "I don't want any more tests."

"But that's the only way to make a diagnosis."

Cassie stared off past Connor, as if the wall behind his head were a window to something horrible. "I've changed my mind. I don't want a diagnosis. I've seen the heme/onc ward ... people with no hair ... vomiting ... no thank you."

Connor had been going over this conversation in his head all morning, trying to anticipate Cassie's reactions so he could consider how to respond. He hadn't anticipated that reaction.

Yesterday, Cassie had practically begged him to evaluate her. Now, she was asking him to stop. But Connor couldn't stop now. Cassie could be in danger.

Cassie stared at her lap for minutes that seemed to

go on forever. Finally she said, "I don't want to have cancer."

Connor put his hand on Cassie's shoulder, the way he'd been taught to do when comforting a patient. But that didn't feel right. It wasn't enough. Connor pulled Cassie into his arms.

Without a moment of hesitation, Cassie wrapped her arms around him and held on tight. As if her life depended on it.

Chapter Six

Before he went to work in the ER, there was something Connor needed do. He had to go back to the old PICU and retrieve the blood drawing supplies that he and Cassie had left there the night before. If someone were to find them, it would arouse suspicion about unauthorized people going into that area and could even prompt an investigation as to what had happened. Connor was pretty sure that no one, not even the custodians, went into the old PICU, but still he wanted to remove the evidence that they were there as soon as possible.

When Connor told Cassie what he was going to do, she said, "I'm going with you." And so the two of them went to the old PICU and snuck back inside. As soon as they entered the main room, Connor stopped in his tracks. The supplies they'd left scattered on top of the nurses' station desk were gone. Connor ran over and checked the floor. There was no trace of them.

Connor's heart pounded. "Who cleaned them up?"

"The ghosts?" Cassie suggested.

Connor half-hoped she was right. If not, that meant someone knew they'd been there.

Cassie marched toward the abandoned patient rooms. "I wonder what fell last night."

"Aren't you worried about the ghosts?" he asked her as he caught up with her.

"When you're going to die, you become a whole lot braver," Cassie responded as she opened the door to one of the rooms.

"You're not going to die, Cassie, not for a long time."

Cassie opened the door to a closet and peered inside. "Chances are I've got leukemia, and I'm *not* doing chemo." Finding nothing, Cassie moved on.

Connor followed her to the next room. "*If* you have leukemia, depending on the type of leukemia, you could have greater than a ninety-five percent chance of achieving remission—"

"And a zero percent chance of staying a doctor," Cassie said as she checked out the closet. "I used to think I'd won some kind of *life lottery*. Getting to be a doctor ... delivering babies ... doing surgery ... stuff other kids, even adults, dream about. It's so much harder to lose something you love than to never have had it at all."

"You're right," Connor said. "And knowing you didn't even try to fight it, I think that would hurt the worst."

Cassie looked at him for a moment—her lips pressed tightly together—and then she left the room. Connor followed her.

As she entered the next room, Cassie suddenly knelt to the floor. "It wasn't a ghost that we heard last night."

On the ground was a small, white kitten. The kitten let out a soft, "Mew," and rubbed against Cassie's hand. Then he rolled onto his back, his tiny paws batting at the air.

"He's so friendly!" Cassie said as she pet his belly.

Connor spotted a small bowl of water and a bowl filled with cat kibble sitting on the countertop. "Someone is taking care of him."

"I wonder if that's who picked up our trash."

"It has to be," Connor said.

But he hoped never to find out.

* * *

Connor's first patient of the day was a three-year-old boy, Timothy. Connor looked over the information that the nurse had entered into the computer about the patient. The boy's mother had bought him to the ER that day because he had pain in his right ear. The boy's vital signs were normal, except that he had a slight fever.

As soon as Connor entered the room, a woman—who Connor presumed was the little boy's mother—told Connor very firmly, "He has an ear infection. He needs antibiotics." The woman's face was tense, angry. "He's been sick for a week. We took him to his doctor two days ago, but the doctor said it was 'just a cold.' Now he has a fever and he's getting sicker. It's not 'just a cold' anymore. I don't know why the doctor didn't put him on antibiotics two days ago. Then we wouldn't be in the ER right now."

Her pale little boy sat sullenly in her lap. His cheerless eyes were partially hidden by his blond, curly hair.

Connor wondered why they hadn't gone back to Timothy's doctor today rather than coming to the ER, but he didn't ask. He didn't want to risk agitating the woman any more than she already was.

"What symptoms is he having?" Connor asked.

"We already told the nurse all that. We've been waiting here for more than four hours. Can't you just look in his ears and give me a prescription?"

"I want to make sure I understand what's going on with him." Connor referred to the nurse's note and continued, "The nurse wrote that he's been having cough and runny nose for a week, and fever and right ear pain for two days? No vomiting or diarrhea?"

"Right," she said, growing more annoyed by the second.

"Has he ever been diagnosed with any medical conditions in the past?"

"Just ear infections," she sighed.

"All right, let's take a look," Connor said, grabbing his stethoscope.

The little boy began to wail, "No shots! No shots!"

"Timothy, I'm not going to give you any shots right now, I'm just going to check you," Connor assured him.

The little boy whimpered and shook his head, unconvinced.

"I pinky swear," Connor said, extending his

pinky. Then he realized that the boy might be too young to know what a pinky swear meant. "That means I promise."

Timothy grabbed hold of Connor's pinky as if he was giving it a hug with his fist and smiled.

"Okay then, can I check you out?" Connor asked.

Timothy nodded and released Connor's finger.

Connor listened to Timothy's chest. The boy's lungs sounded clear, but Connor heard an unusual galloping heart murmur. Connor pressed his fingers into Timothy's belly and immediately noticed a large lump on the left side that shouldn't be there. His mind raced with possible causes for the mass as he continued examining the little boy, trying to hide his growing alarm. He felt the boy's glands and checked his mouth and his nose. Finally, Connor slid a small scope into Timothy's ears, one at a time. The left ear was normal, but on the right side, instead of a pearly, relaxed eardrum, Connor found a bulging, red eardrum that had two blisters on it.

As Connor pulled out the scope, Timothy's mother asked, "Did you really need to do all that just to figure out he has an ear infection?"

"Yes—" Connor had done the exam he'd been

taught to do on any patient who has a fever. In most cases, the exam is normal with the exception of an ear infection, a throat infection, pneumonia, or wheezing, but in Timothy's case, what Connor had found on the exam was very concerning.

"Does he have an infection?" she asked.

"Yes, he does, but—"

The woman stared at Connor. "So his doctor missed it?"

"Not necessarily," Connor answered. "The ear infection might not have been there two days ago."

"All right, fine, which antibiotic are you going to give him?"

Connor sat down on the stool. Yes, Timothy had an ear infection, and they would treat it, but there was something potentially much more serious going on.

"There's something else we need to discuss," Connor said.

The woman clenched her jaw and her face reddened. She seemed about ready to explode. "What else could we *possibly* need to discuss?"

"When I examined Timothy, I felt a mass in his belly."

The color drained from the woman's face. "A

mass?"

"A lump," Connor clarified.

The woman's eyes narrowed. "Maybe one of the grown-up doctors should examine him."

If any patient at Westley Hospital requested to see an adult doctor, their request was always granted. This policy was put in place mostly for the patients' piece of mind. To that day, none of these second opinions had ever differed from the Kid Doc's initial assessment. Connor felt certain about what he'd discovered on Timothy's exam, but after his experience with Mr. Peterson, he was almost glad to have a second opinion.

"Doctor Mark Hansen will be right in," Connor said, and he got up and left the room.

Connor found his dad at a computer in the ER doctor's room, where he was reviewing patients' charts.

"Dad, the parent of one of my patients has requested a second opinion," Connor said.

His dad logged off the computer and turned to him. "Tell me about the patient."

"Timothy is a three-year-old boy with a one week history of URI symptoms and two days of fever and right ear pain. On exam, he has right bullous myringitis—"

"Sounds pretty straight forward," his dad said, rising from his chair. "Why do you think they asked to see me?"

"He also has a left upper quadrant mass," Connor said.

Mark frowned and inhaled deeply. "Okay, what tests do you want to order?"

Connor rattled off the lab tests that he thought Timothy should have done to help diagnose his condition, "CBC, CMP, PT, PTT, uric acid, LDH, and a blood culture. We should also do a UA, micro, and culture. And we'll need a CT chest, abdomen, and pelvis."

"Go ahead and order all that," Mark said. "What room is Timothy in?"

"Three," Connor answered.

"I'll be back." Mark left the room.

As Connor signed into the computer to order the tests and studies for Timothy, Hannah entered the room.

"Hey, Hannah," Connor said.

"Hey," Hannah responded without looking at him.

"How's your OR patient from last night?" Connor asked. He was sure Hannah had gone to the ICU that morning, before her shift in the ER, to check on the patient. Hannah always followed up on her patients, even after they were no longer her responsibility.

"She's doing well," Hannah answered curtly.

"Good," Connor said, wondering why Hannah seemed so upset.

"While I was in the ICU, I checked to see how Mr. Peterson is doing—"

Connor tensed. "How is he?"

"The ICU docs extubated him early this morning, and they said he was asking about you."

Connor's heart beat against his ribs. "What did he say?"

"Just that he wanted to talk to you," Hannah said, and then she left the room.

Connor's heart pounded harder and harder and harder.

He knew exactly what Mr. Peterson wanted to talk about.

* * *

Two hours later, Connor' pager beeped and displayed

the extension for the radiology department. Connor assumed that the radiologist was calling to discuss Timothy's results. Timothy was the only patient he'd sent for x-rays so far that day.

As he dialed the phone, dread filling his chest, he pulled up Timothy's x-ray images on the computer.

A woman answered the phone, "Radiology."

"It's Doctor Connor, I was paged."

"Yes, please hold for Doctor Kelly."

While he waited, Connor scrolled through the gray and white virtual slices of Timothy's body. Inside Timothy's belly, where the light-grey, bean-shaped, left kidney should be, there was a large, oval lump filled with different shades of darker gray.

As Connor stared at the ominous image, a girl's voice came on the line. "Connor, it's Kelly." Connor knew Doctor Kelly. He'd spoken to her many times before. Usually, her tone was quite chipper, but this time it was low and serious. "I'm calling about Timothy Dow, medical record number: 4753804. On the CT chest, abdomen, and pelvis there is a left-sided, heterogeneous, intrarenal mass consistent with Wilms' tumor …"

Connor's stomach felt as if it had twisted on itself.

Although he was listening to Doctor Kelly describe the details of the scan, Connor's thoughts were already racing far ahead. In a few minutes, he would have to go back to Timothy's room, and sit with Ms. Dow, and tell her that her child was very sick.

Her three-year-old little boy had cancer.

Chapter Seven

When Connor reentered Timothy's room, Mrs. Dow was almost unrecognizable. Her eyelids were puffy and red, and her face was so creased with worry that she looked as if she had aged ten years in just a few hours. Timothy was wrapped in a hospital blanket, asleep on her lap.

The Kid Docs are taught that, when giving bad news to patients and families, they should get to the point quickly. And so Connor sat down on the stool, and looked at Mrs. Dow and said, "Timothy's CT scan showed that he has a tumor in his left kidney. Based on the information we have at this point, it's likely that he has Wilms' Tumor, a type of kidney cancer."

Mrs. Dow covered her face with her hands and cried without making a sound. Connor placed his hand on her shoulder, unsure whether she would let it stay there, but she did.

Mrs. Dow spoke without looking up, "Yesterday, we flew in from Michigan to visit my parents. My father is in hospice. I wanted Timothy to see his grandfather before he passed away."

That explained why they hadn't gone to Timothy's doctor today. Timothy's doctor was halfway across the country.

Suddenly, Mrs. Dow's body went from wilted to tense, as if someone had flipped a switch.

"How long has that tumor been growing inside of Timothy?" she asked, her voice angry.

"It's hard to say for sure," Connor said.

"But it was there two days ago?"

"Yes."

"Timothy's doctor didn't check his belly the other day. He just looked in his ears and said he was fine. Timothy has *cancer*, and his doctor said he was *fine*," she said, shaking her head.

Yes, Timothy's doctor had missed the tumor but … "Even if his doctor had discovered the tumor two days ago, it's unlikely that it would have made any difference in Timothy's outcome," Connor explained.

Mrs. Dow's eyes widened. "Timothy's *outcome*? Is he going to die?"

"We don't have enough information to give a prognosis yet. The first step is an excisional biopsy. A surgeon will remove the tumor and a pathologist will evaluate the tissue to make an exact diagnosis. That will help guide Timothy's treatment."

"What kind of treatment?"

"That depends on the diagnosis. You can rest assured that we will carefully transfer Timothy's care to his doctor and the specialists in Michigan so that he can receive the best care possible."

"I want him to have his treatment here."

* * *

About an hour later, Timothy and his mother departed for the oncology floor, where cancer specialists would begin treating him. On their way out of the ER, Mrs. Dow stopped to thank Connor for taking care of her son. Timothy was sitting in a child-sized wheelchair, smiling and shouting, "Vroom! Vroom!" to the nurse who had been pushing him along. The little boy didn't have any idea that he had cancer or what that even meant.

It was time for Connor's lunch break, but instead of going to the doctors' cafeteria, Connor headed up to the ICU to talk with Mr. Peterson. Dread filled Connor's lungs, crowding out the oxygen, making him breathe twice as fast. He didn't want to see Mr.

Peterson's broken body, because he knew that every scratch was his fault.

When Connor entered the ICU, Doctor Robin—who was the same year as Connor—spotted him. "Hi, Connor, what brings you to the ICU?" Robin asked.

"I came to see Mr. Peterson."

"He's doing great!" Robin beamed. "We have him off all of his pressors. Should be able to transfer him out tomorrow."

Mr. Peterson was doing well. Connor felt a little less guilty.

Robin added, "He's in Room Ten."

"Thanks," Connor said, and he slowly walked toward Mr. Peterson's room.

Through the glass walls of Room Ten, Connor could see Mr. Peterson in the bed. He was alone, reading a book. Both of his thighs were wrapped in thick dressings. Surgical nails attached to metal rods stuck out from the dressings. The ends of these nails were deep inside Mr. Peterson's thighs, holding the pieces of his broken bones in position while he healed. Tubes and wires connected Mr. Peterson to pumps and monitors. Connor couldn't believe that—according to Doctor Robin—Mr. Peterson was doing *great*. To

Connor he looked like he was doing *okay* at best. Most non-doctor people would have said that Mr. Peterson looked *awful*. Connor's guilt grew stronger than ever. He reluctantly tapped on the door.

"Doctor Connor," Mr. Peterson said. His voice was scratchy, probably because of the breathing tube that had, until that morning, been down his throat. "I wanted to talk to you."

"I heard," Connor said.

And then Mr. Peterson paused for a very long time. Connor wondered whether he should say something, but Mr. Peterson was studying his bedside table as if he were collecting his thoughts and so Connor just stood there, waiting.

Finally Mr. Peterson said, "If it wasn't for you, I wouldn't be here."

Connor wanted to say he was sorry. He wanted to tell Mr. Peterson that he wished he could have prevented the horrible car accident that had left him so terribly injured.

Mr. Peterson continued, "If it wasn't for you, Doctor Connor, I'd be dead."

Connor was confused. "What?"

"The day I met you, my wife had dragged me to

the emergency room. I was sure the chest pain that I was having was nothing serious. But you told me there might be something wrong with my heart. I didn't want to believe you, but a little part of me *did* believe you. The day after I saw you, I had that pain again, only it was much worse. I felt like I couldn't breathe. I figured it was probably just something I ate, but I remembered what you said and thought I'd better get it checked out. So I jumped into my car and headed back to the ER. My heart stopped on the way there. I passed out and crashed the car. I know you said that if I ever had chest pain again I should call an ambulance, but I didn't want to make a big deal about it." He eyed the machines, tubes, and wires attached to him, and sighed. "Guess I ended up making a big deal about it anyway."

Mr. Peterson's eyes filled with tears. "Thankfully no one else was hurt in the accident. I wouldn't have been able to forgive myself if that had happened." He wiped his eyes with the back of his hand. "Thing is … I was alone at my office when the pain started. If I had just taken some antacid and rested on the couch, it would have been hours before they found me … dead. My kids would have lost their daddy."

Mr. Peterson began paging through the jumbled pile of papers on his bedside table. "I have something for you," he said, "and also for the doctor who got my heart started again with the paddles."

"I did that," Connor said quietly. "I was your doctor after the accident too."

Mr. Peterson studied Connor's face. "You were?"

Connor nodded.

"Then these are *both* for you." He handed Connor two papers. Crayon drawings. One showed a stick-figure doctor listening to a seated man's chest with a stethoscope. The other showed a doctor zapping a man's chest with two things that looked like ping-pong paddles. "My daughter made them."

"Thank you," Connor said, feeling his eyes moisten.

"No. Thank *you*, Doctor Connor," Mr. Peterson said. "Thank you for saving my life. Twice."

* * *

Just as Connor returned to the ER to start his afternoon of work, Nurse Mike poked his head into the doctors' room and said, "I need a doc to go up to the helipad."

That meant that a patient was arriving at the

hospital by helicopter. An ER doctor and nurse needed to meet the patient on the hospital roof and accompany them to the ER, just in case the patient needed any treatment along the way. Patients who arrive at the hospital by helicopter are usually very sick. They come by helicopter because they might not survive a long ambulance ride to the hospital, even if the ambulance raced there with lights and sirens blaring.

"I'll do it," Connor said.

He caught up with Nurse Mike, who was wheeling an empty ER gurney toward the elevator, and asked him, "What's coming in?"

"We don't have a lot of info on this one," Nurse Mike said. "They were flying in from way out in the mountains and were having radio trouble. It sounded like an adult male in cardiac arrest."

A man whose heart has stopped.

Mike smiled. "In other news, I hear you have a girlfriend."

"Who said that?" Connor asked, trying to hide his horror.

"A little bird," Mike said.

"Hannah?"

"Yup," Mike said. "She said your girlfriend is an

obstetrician. Funny, I always thought you and *Hannah* would eventually get together."

"Eww."

"Why not? She's cute."

"I don't know. It would be weird," Connor said. "How dare Hannah tell rumors about me!"

"So it's just a rumor?" Mike asked.

"I have a new *friend* who's a *girl*. That's all."

"You sure?"

"Not really," Connor admitted. "I know we're friends. But I think she might want to be my girlfriend. And don't know how to find out."

"Do you want her to be your girlfriend?" Mike asked.

"I think so. What do you think I should do?"

All of the female nurses loved Mike. Maybe he would have some helpful ideas.

"First of all, there's no rush. Until you're sure how you feel, just be her friend. And if you *do* decide that you want her to be your girlfriend, be honest. When it comes to guys and girls and relationships, a lot of people play games. Not fun games, stupid games. Usually they pretend not to like someone when they really do. If you're honest about how you feel, and she cares about you, she'll admire your honesty. If she doesn't then, believe me, you really don't want her to be your girlfriend."

They arrived at the elevator bank where a security officer was waiting for them. He scanned their ID badges, swiped his badge in a card reader inside the elevator, and then pushed the button for the roof.

Connor, Mike, and the security officer stood silently in the elevator as it climbed fifteen floors. The doors opened on the roof, and Connor and Mike stepped out with their gurney to await the helicopter. As they did, Connor caught a glimpse of wavy red hair disappearing behind a wall. He was sure it was Cassie. He wanted to call out to her, but of course he didn't.

Mike took in the view. "I love coming up here!"

"Yeah," Connor agreed. "Me too."

Mike had no idea how often Connor snuck up onto the roof.

"Here they come," Mike said, pointing to a tiny dot in the sky.

As the dot grew larger, the sound of the helicopter's spinning blades rapidly went from distant to deafening. Stormy winds engulfed them as the chopper came in for a landing. Connor and Mike had to hold down the gurney's pad and sheets so they didn't fly away.

The back door to the helicopter popped open. It was time to meet his patient.

Chapter Eight

"Fifty-three-year-old male status post cardiac arrest," a female paramedic shouted to Connor above the whoosh of the helicopter. "Received bystander CPR and AED defibrillation attempt times one prior to our arrival at the scene. On our monitor, patient was in pulseless v-tach …"

Connor peered inside the helicopter at his patient. The man didn't look nearly as sick as the patient the paramedic was describing. Now, the patient was sitting up on the helicopter gurney, arguing with a male paramedic who was trying to secure a safety belt around the man.

The female paramedic reached over and buckled the man's safety belt—ending the argument—and then she continued, "We gave him epi and amiodarone along with two additional defibrillation attempts. After the second shock, he converted to sinus rhythm."

The male paramedic hopped out of the helicopter and grabbed hold of the plastic board that held the patient. "Ready?" he asked everyone. "On my count.

One, two, three."

Mike assisted the paramedics in depositing the patient on the ER gurney. Then a boy—who looked about Alex's age—jumped out of the helicopter followed by the female paramedic.

Everyone made their way down the walkway and into the open elevator.

When the elevator doors closed, the patient turned to Mike. "Doc, I need to get back to my ranch."

"I'm a nurse," Mike replied.

"Where's the doctor?" the man asked, scanning the faces surrounding his gurney.

"I'm right here," Connor said.

The man looked at Connor. His forehead creased. "How old are you?"

"Fourteen," Connor replied.

"Dad, they took you to Westley Hospital," the teenaged boy said.

The man turned to the paramedics. "Why didn't you take me to a *real* hospital?"

His son answered, "This is a real hospital. And it's won all kinds of awards."

Connor glanced at the paramedics' clipboard to learn his patient's name, then he said, "Mr. North, we'll take very good care of you here."

Mr. North looked at Connor through narrowed eyes, and then he said, "Bob. My name is Bob."

The elevator doors opened, and they moved into the busy hallway, headed toward the ER. As they walked, Connor gathered information about his patient.

"Do you have any medical problems?" he asked.

"High blood pressure," Mr. North answered.

"Are you taking any medications?"

"No, I don't believe in medications."

"Have you ever had a heart attack before?"

"A little one."

Mr. North's son turned to his father, his jaw agape. "You did?"

"Aaron, I didn't tell you because I didn't want to worry you," Mr. North said to his son. "Who's back at the ranch? I need you to call them and make sure Ming's okay. The last thing I remember, I was in the arena with her."

"Ming's fine. She was in the holding area when we left," Aaron said.

Mr. North shook his head in disbelief. "Ming hates the holding area. I've never been able to get her to go in there. Who got Ming into the holding area?"

"Who's Ming?" Connor asked, curious.

"One of my tigers," Mr. North said.

"You have tigers?" Connor was certain that Mr. North was just confused.

"Yes," Mr. North said, "and bears, lions, leopards, and elephants."

Connor looked to Aaron for confirmation. Aaron nodded vigorously, and so did the paramedics.

Mr. North continued, "So you see why I need to get back to my ranch."

"Leslie's taking care of the animals," Aaron assured Mr. North, "and she's calling the other trainers to come help. Everything's under control."

"I need to get back to my ranch before dark," Mr. North persisted. "Can we make this quick, Doc?"

Anxiety squeezed Connor's stomach. His patient didn't seem to understand the seriousness of what had happened. What if Mr. North tried to leave the hospital without proper evaluation? This patient could end up in the same situation as Mr. Peterson, or worse.

"Mr. North," Connor said, trying to keep his voice from shaking, "earlier today your heart stopped beating. If it wasn't for CPR, powerful medications, and multiple defibrillations of your heart, right now you'd be dead. You are *extremely* lucky to be alive. If we send you back home without appropriate care, it is only a matter of time before your heart stops again. And next time you might not be so lucky."

Mr. North laid his head back onto the gurney and closed his eyes. He took a slow, deep breath, and then he said, "Bob. My name is Bob."

* * *

As soon as the paramedics parked Mr. North's gurney in the center of Trauma Room Two, the ER nurses, who had been awaiting the patient's arrival, sprang into action.

Connor placed his stethoscope on Mr. North's chest. "Take a deep breath for me," he told his patient.

"I need to place another IV line and draw some blood," Nurse Samantha said to Mr. North. "You're going to feel a little poke."

Mr. North kept his eyes closed, but he breathed when Connor asked him to and cooperated with the nurses. Aaron stood a few steps away, fidgeting anxiously.

When Connor finished his exam, he said to Mr.

North, "We're going to do some tests and x-rays. I'll be back to check on you soon, but if you need me before then, just let the nurses know."

"Thank you." Mr. North opened his eyes—just for a second—when he said that and then promptly closed them again.

Connor went off to the ER doctors' room. As he stepped inside, his body tensed. Hannah was sitting at one of the computers, examining CT scan images of someone's brain. She glanced up when Connor entered and gave him a restrained smile. Hannah was the last person on Earth who he wanted to see. He was furious at her, and she seemed to sense it.

"What do you think of this scan?" Hannah asked him, gesturing to the images on her computer screen.

Connor forced himself to focus on the x-ray images. "What's the patient's history?" he asked her.

"Two-year-old male. Fell out of a second story window onto dirt. He looks great on exam."

Connor carefully looked over the virtual slices through the little boy's head and then said, "I don't see any midline shift or signs of intracranial hemorrhage, but I'd run it by radiology just to be sure."

"I paged them, but they haven't called me back

yet," Hannah said.

Connor didn't say anything in response. He sat down at another computer and stared at the login screen, anger at Hannah boiling through him. He couldn't restrain it any longer. "Hannah, did you tell people that I have a girlfriend?"

Hannah's eyes darted from her computer, to the floor, to Connor. Connor could tell that she knew she'd been caught. Hannah never lied, so Connor was pretty sure she'd admit it.

Hannah crossed her arms in front of herself. "Well, you *do*."

Connor shook his head, frustration burning inside his chest. "You don't know that. You don't know *anything* about that."

"I know what I saw," Hannah said.

"You saw my *friend* on an ER gurney," Connor said. "I was helping her. I would have helped you the same way ... back when we were friends."

Hannah's forehead furrowed. "We're not friends anymore?"

"*Friends* don't start rumors about each other."

"It's *not* a rumor if it's true," Hannah insisted.

"It's *not* true," Connor said through a clenched

jaw. "She's not my girlfriend."

"But I saw …"

"What?" Connor asked. "What do you *think* you saw?"

Hannah stood up, blinking rapidly as tears filled her eyes. She glanced at Connor for a moment before she said, "Never mind. I'm going to go down to radiology. Not that *you* care." And then she left.

Connor exhaled and turned back to his computer, his anger now replaced with guilt about upsetting Hannah. Deep down, Connor knew that she was probably right about Cassie being his girlfriend. At least he thought so. And hoped so.

But why did Hannah care so much?

Connor typed his password into the computer and forced himself to focus on his job, trying not to think about Hannah.

* * *

Mr. North's blood test results came back, and Connor was able to confirm his preliminary diagnosis. Now he knew for sure that Mr. North had had a heart attack. There were other minor abnormalities on his lab tests, but Connor saw nothing serious, until he pulled up Mr.

North's chest x-ray on the computer. Even though he wasn't a radiologist, Connor immediately spotted a problem. Mr. North had an ominous, gray spot in his right lung, about the size of a dime. A spot that shouldn't be there. A spot that could be cancer.

"Connor, Mr. North is crashing!" Nurse Mike shouted into the doctors' room.

Connor jumped up and ran to Trauma Room Two. Mr. North lay lifeless on his gurney. Nurse Samantha was pressing on his chest, pumping his heart.

"What happened?" Connor asked. He almost couldn't believe that the patient who, just one hour ago, was adamant about being discharged as soon as possible was now close to death.

"He went into v-fib," Nurse Samantha said. "We defibrillated him once at two-hundred joules."

"Hold CPR," Connor ordered. "Let's do a rhythm check."

Samantha stopped pressing on Mr. North's chest.

Connor checked the monitor and swallowed. "Still v-fib."

Samantha started pushing on Mr. North's chest again.

"Give him an amp of epi," Connor said.

Nurse Mike pulled open a drawer on the red crash cart that held medicines and equipment used to save dying patients. He took out two syringes and quickly emptied the contents into one of Mr. North's IV lines. "Epi's in," Mike announced when he was through.

"Charge to three hundred," Connor said.

An ER nurse turned a dial and pushed a button on the defibrillator. The machine made its long, loud, high-pitched, awful sound.

Connor grabbed the paddles from the defibrillator and placed them on Mr. North's chest. "Clear," he shouted. He held the paddles down firmly as Mr. North's body jumped, and then he said, "Resume CPR."

"Please don't let him die!" Aaron pleaded.

"I'll do everything I can," Connor said. He couldn't even begin to imagine what it was like for Aaron to watch his dad dying. Connor thought about what it would be like to see his own dad on the gurney. The thought made him shudder.

Connor turned to Mike, "I'm going to intubate." He grabbed a scope from a nearby tray and eased it deep into Mr. North's mouth, pushing the man's thick tongue out of the way to reveal his delicate, pink vocal cords. Carefully, Connor slid a breathing tube into place. "I'm in."

Mike listened to Mr. North's chest. "Breath sounds equal," he said, confirming that the tube had been properly inserted.

All of a sudden, Mr. North's big hand came to life. It rose up, grabbed hold of the tube that Connor had just placed into his throat, and yanked the tube right out.

"What the heck?" Mr. North mumbled as he tried to get up.

Aaron ran to his father, his relieved face wet with tears. "Lie down, Dad. The doctors and nurses are helping you."

Mr. North handed the breathing tube to Connor, staring at the thing with disgust. "I think I've had enough help for now."

Connor couldn't help smiling. His patient, who had been dying moments before, seemed just fine.

But then Connor's stomach twisted.

Mr. North wasn't fine.

Mr. North had a mass in his lung.

Chapter Nine

"Sixteen-year-old female. Severe abdominal pain," a paramedic reported to Connor as he wheeled an ambulance gurney into Trauma Room Three. "I'm thinking she's in labor," he added.

"Owww … I am … NOT … owww … pregnant!" the girl said to the paramedic, as if he were the biggest idiot on the planet.

Connor thought that the paramedic had made a reasonable assumption, although there were certainly other possibilities.

"I'm going to need an ultrasound," Connor said to Nurse Samantha. Then he turned to his patient. "I'm Doctor Connor. What's your name?"

"Lisa … owwwww … Can you … make … owwwww … the pain … owwwww … stop?"

"How long have you been having pain?" Connor asked her.

"Since I … woke up."

Connor pressed lightly on Lisa's chubby belly with his fingertips. It was difficult to tell for sure, but he was fairly certain that he felt a firm mass filling most of her abdomen. Although he hadn't examined many pregnant bellies before, he was pretty sure that Lisa was, in fact, pregnant.

The ultrasound technician rushed in the door with his machine.

"That was fast!" Connor remarked.

"I was just finishing up next door," the technician said.

Connor glanced through the big window into Trauma Room Four. Cassie was there consulting with a pregnant patient.

When Connor looked back at Lisa, the ultrasound technician had already started his exam.

"How many weeks are you?" the technician asked Lisa.

"Weeks what?" she asked. Her pain seemed to have lessened.

"Pregnant," the technician said.

"I am not pregnant!" Lisa shouted.

The technician turned a dial on the ultrasound machine, and a fast *whoosh, whoosh, whoosh* could be heard—the sound of a baby's heartbeat.

"Baby looks full term," the technician said to

Connor.

Connor turned to Lisa. "I'm going to have an obstetrician evaluate you, then we'll move you up to the labor and delivery floor."

Lisa shook her head, tears falling from her eyes, as she stared at the fuzzy gray image of her baby on the ultrasound monitor. "I don't want to deliver anything. I just want to go home."

Nurse Samantha put a gentle hand on Lisa's shoulder. "That's not an option."

"My mom is going to kill me," Lisa said, slamming the back of her head against the gurney.

Out of the corner of his eye, Connor saw Cassie walking out of Trauma Room Four.

"Excuse me a minute," Connor said to Lisa. He dashed out of the room and caught up with Cassie in the hallway. "Hey, Cassie!"

Cassie turned toward him, and Connor found himself standing a little too close to her, but neither of them stepped away.

"How are you doing?" Connor whispered.

"Fine," Cassie said, but she looked worried, vulnerable.

Connor swallowed, feeling awkward. "I've got a

patient for you."

She nodded, suddenly transforming into a self-assured, confident doctor. "Tell me about her."

"Sixteen-year-old female. Full term. Crampy abdominal pain since awakening today. I think she's in labor."

"You're probably right." Cassie started after Connor into Trauma Room Three. "What's her name?" she asked him.

"Lisa," Connor said.

Cassie walked up to the gurney. "Lisa, I'm Doctor Cassie. Is it okay if I examine you?"

"Go ahead," Lisa sighed.

Cassie pulled on a sterile glove and reached under Lisa's blanket.

Lisa's face contorted uncomfortably until Cassie pulled out her hand. "You're five centimeters dilated," Cassie told Lisa. "If you'd like, I can order an epidural to minimize your pain."

"Physical or emotional?" Lisa asked.

Cassie put her hand on Lisa's arm. "Physical, but we'll work on the emotional stuff too, okay?"

"Okay," Lisa said.

Cassie gave her a warm smile. "I'll page the

anesthesiologist."

As she stepped away from the bed, Cassie said to Nurse Samantha, "I think we just filled our last bed upstairs. We might need to keep her in ER for a little bit."

"No problem," Samantha said.

Cassie turned to Connor and said softly, "If I get tied up, you know how to deliver babies now, right?" A look of fear must have crossed Connor's face because Cassie quickly added, "Just kidding." And then she lightly brushed the top of Connor's hand with her fingers, sending a warm tingling through his entire body.

Connor watched Cassie leave, feeling sadness weigh down his body. He had to figure out some way to convince Cassie to have more blood drawn for the tests that Doctor Keith had recommended. Cassie needed a diagnosis. Before it was too late.

* * *

As Connor typed into one of the ER doctors' room computers, he couldn't stop thinking about Cassie. She had sworn him to secrecy. He couldn't tell anyone what was going on with her. But he needed advice. He needed help trying to figure out what to do.

Connor turned to Mark, who was reviewing charts at a nearby computer. "Dad, what would happen if one of the Kid Docs got sick? Like with cancer or something."

"We would make sure you were treated by the best doctors in the country," he said without looking away from the screen.

Connor thought that his dad sounded like he did when he was being interviewed on TV, like he was hiding something important.

"But what about working as a doctor?" Connor asked. "Could they still do that?"

"If they had cancer?"

"Or anything like that."

"Well, in the case of cancer, during certain stages of the disease and the therapy, the immune system can become severely suppressed. Working in the hospital, with so many potential sources of infection, would be dangerous."

"But once they were treated and in remission, could they work as a doctor?" Connor asked.

Mark turned away from the computer screen and searched Connor's face for a moment, then he asked,

"We're not just playing 'what if' are we?" Without waiting for a response, he continued, "Who's sick, Connor?"

"To tell you would break doctor-patient confidentiality," Connor said.

"You're not their doctor. You're their friend."

Even though he knew that he was about to get in a lot of trouble, Connor said, "I performed the examination and ordered the blood tests. I *am* their doctor."

"Was someone supervising you?"

It was required that an adult doctor be assigned to the care of every patient treated by a Kid Doc. Often the adult doctor did nothing more than review the patient's chart, but they were always available to examine the patient and answer any questions. This was not just his dad's rule, this was the law.

"No," Connor said.

Mark's face tensed. "You cannot treat each other without supervision."

"I consulted oncology. I'm doing everything I would do for any other patient," Connor said. "The oncologist suggested further evaluation, but the patient is refusing. They're scared."

"Are they neutropenic?" Mark asked.

"No," Connor said.

"Toxic?"

"Not at all."

Mark exhaled. "As of this moment, *I* am your supervising doctor. *I* am ultimately responsible for this patient. You have twenty-four hours to have the tests completed to make a definitive diagnosis. Meanwhile, you need to monitor the patient closely. If anything changes, I need to know immediately."

At least for the moment, his dad wasn't punishing him. Instead, he had placed his full trust in him. Connor still had no idea how to convince Cassie to continue with the evaluation, but he said, "Okay."

"I want you to review the danger signs with the oncologist. This isn't your area of expertise. Your patient could become extremely ill, very quickly—"

Connor's pager beeped. It was a stat page to Trauma Room Three. A stat page meant he was needed right away. His patient was in serious trouble.

* * *

Nurse Samantha met Connor in the trauma room doorway. "Lisa's having late decels," she said, sounding concerned.

"What are late decels?" Connor asked.

"The baby's heart rate is dropping after each contraction and taking a long time to come back up to normal. Late decels can indicate that the baby is not getting enough oxygen. I positioned Lisa on her side and put her on one hundred percent oxygen via face mask, but the decels have persisted."

"Did you stat page Cassie?" Connor didn't know much about how to treat patients who were in labor, especially when something was going horribly wrong.

"Yes, she's on her way," Samantha said.

Good, Connor thought. He walked over to Lisa's bed and looked at her monitors. At the moment, Lisa was in between contractions and the baby's heart rate was reassuringly fast, normal for such a tiny baby.

"How are you feeling, Lisa?" Connor asked.

"That epi-whatever-thing that they gave me is working," she said, referring to the numbing medicine that the anesthesia doctor had injected into Lisa's spinal column. "The contractions aren't nearly as bad as before. But Samantha said the baby's heart rate is too slow."

"Right now it's normal, but it has been slowing

down with your contractions," Connor said. "We're going to have the obstetrician check you. She's on her way."

Connor hoped that Cassie would get here soon. Even though everything seemed fine now, the problem could return with Lisa's next contraction. While he waited, Connor listened to Lisa's heart and lungs. They sounded normal. He continued listening and watching the monitor until Cassie rushed into the room.

"What's going on?" Cassie asked.

"The baby was having late decels," Connor said.

Cassie scrolled through the monitor readings on the computer and then said to Lisa, "I need to check your cervix again." She pulled on a glove and slid her hand under Lisa's blanket. Almost as soon as she began her exam, she turned urgently to Samantha. "The cord's prolapsed," she said in a quiet voice. "Put her in Trendelenberg, then call upstairs and tell them I need an OR for a stat C-section."

Samantha lowered the head of Lisa's bed and then hurried to the phone.

Cassie turned back to her patient. "Your baby's umbilical cord has slipped out of the uterus. The baby is showing signs of distress. You need to deliver as soon as possible."

"I need to push?" Lisa asked.

"No, you're not fully dilated. We need to perform the delivery surgically."

Lisa started to cry. "I've never had surgery."

"Lisa!" a woman shouted as she raced from the doorway to the gurney.

"Mom!" Lisa appeared relieved and worried at the same time.

Cassie turned to the woman. "I'm Doctor Cassie, and this is Doctor Connor."

"I'm Mrs. Ryan, Lisa's mother—" the woman started.

"They want me to have surgery, Mom," Lisa said, tears falling down her cheeks.

"Does she have appendicitis?" Lisa's mother asked.

"No," Lisa said. "I'm … I'm pregnant."

Mrs. Ryan shook her head. "Oh, no, no, no, no."

Cassie added, "She's full term and in labor, but the umbilical cord has fallen into the birth canal, compromising the baby's blood supply. I recommend that we perform an emergency Caesarean section."

"I don't want to have surgery, Mom," Lisa said.

"Is surgery the only option?" Mrs. Ryan asked.

"I think it is the best way to protect the health of the baby," Cassie said.

"Go ahead and do the surgery," Mrs. Ryan said.

"I'm sorry, but Lisa needs to consent," Cassie said.

"She's a child," Mrs. Ryan told Cassie. "She's only sixteen years old."

"But she's pregnant," Cassie said. "Legally, that makes her—"

"That's ridiculous—" Mrs. Ryan started.

Lisa spoke up, "What will happen to the baby if I don't have the surgery?"

Cassie sat down on the stool next to Lisa's gurney. "It is possible that lack of oxygen could cause permanent damage to the baby's brain, or even death. But the surgery carries some significant risks to *you*. You could develop a serious infection, life-threatening bleeding, blood clots, or other complications that can be fatal—"

"I consent," Lisa said softly, her face wrinkling with pain. The monitor indicated that she was starting another contraction.

"Are you sure?" Cassie asked.

"Yes," Lisa said, her voice stronger.

Cassie turned to Samantha. "Call upstairs and let them know we're on our way."

Samantha went to the phone.

As Cassie explained the next steps to Lisa and her mother, Lisa's monitor began to alarm. The baby's heart rate was dropping again.

Samantha rushed over and said to Cassie, "They won't have any OR's available for at least thirty minutes."

Cassie shook her head, her eyes fixed on the monitor as she lowered the head of Lisa's bed even further. "We can't wait that long. Tell them to send down an OB pack and whatever staff they have. We can do it here."

Connor had a sinking feeling that "we" was going to include *him*.

* * *

Cassie sliced into Lisa's belly with a scalpel. An OR nurse dabbed the blood away with gauze. Because this was an emergency surgery, everything was happening quickly.

Lisa was awake, but she was lying motionless beneath blue sheets that covered her entire body except for her belly. The anesthesiologist had injected more numbing medicine around Lisa's spinal cord, and so she didn't feel the cutting of her belly at all.

Lisa's mother sat on a stool nearby, wearing blue scrubs like the ones doctors and nurses wear in the operating room. Doctor Peter—a Twelfth Year Kid Doc who was a neonatologist—waited with Hannah by a small table set under a heating lamp, ready to take care of Lisa's baby.

Connor stood facing Cassie, with Lisa's belly between the two of them. The OR nurse handed him a metal suction tube attached to a long hose.

"Get ready to suction," Cassie said to Connor.

Clear fluid gushed out, like a tiny fountain, as Cassie cut into Lisa's uterus with the scalpel. Connor sucked up the fluid as fast as he could. Cassie made the cut in Lisa's uterus bigger, and Connor sucked up more fluid. Then Cassie reached inside.

"You're going to feel some pressure," Cassie said to Lisa.

Suddenly, the baby's head popped into view. Cassie reached under the shoulders and pulled the infant from Lisa's body. It looked like it took every bit of Cassie's strength to do so.

"It's a boy," Cassie announced, raising him up to let Lisa and Mrs. Ryan have a look at him.

The tiny baby cried weakly.

Lisa pulled the oxygen mask away from her face. "Why is he so blue?" she asked.

"You were a little blue when you were born," Mrs. Ryan said to Lisa.

Cassie passed the baby to Connor. "Get him to the warmer." Something about the way she said that made Connor think that something was very wrong with the infant.

Clutching the baby to his chest, Connor quickly walked to Hannah and Peter. He placed the baby onto the heated blankets in front of them.

Peter instantly went to work, drying off the floppy infant. With a skinny, flexible suction tube, he removed fluid from the baby's mouth and nose, then he rubbed the baby's back. The baby was breathing, but he wasn't crying. His skin remained a dusky blue-purple color.

"What's his pulse?" Peter asked Hannah.

Hannah gently squeezed the baby's umbilical

cord. A few seconds later, she said, "Pulse is one twenty." The baby's heart rate was perfectly normal.

Peter grabbed a stethoscope. "Give him oxygen. Put him on an oximeter," he ordered urgently.

As Peter listened to the baby's chest, Hannah placed a small oxygen mask over the baby's face. Connor stared at the little blue infant. Blue skin meant that the baby didn't have enough oxygen in his blood. *But what was the problem?*

Peter lifted the stethoscope from the baby's chest and eyed the oximeter readout. "Looks like congenital heart disease," he said, somber.

Connor remembered a magazine article he'd once read. It told the story of one of Alex's patients, a girl who was born with a malformed heart. Until Alex performed the risky, delicate surgery to fix her heart, her skin was blue. In the magazine, there was a photo of the baby that had been taken before the surgery. Lisa's baby looked just like the baby in that photo.

Lisa's baby had a broken heart.

* * *

It had been about thirty minutes since Doctor Peter placed Lisa's blue baby inside a clear capsule—to keep him warm during his trip to the neonatal intensive care unit—and whisked him out of Trauma Room Three. Cassie had just finished sewing up Lisa's belly when Peter reentered the room.

Lisa looked at the empty table under the heating lamp, then she turned to Peter and asked weakly, "When are you bringing my baby back?"

"He needs to stay in the neonatal intensive care unit—" Peter started.

"Why? What's wrong with him?" Lisa asked.

"Your baby has a heart defect called transposition of the great vessels," Peter said.

Lisa's forehead creased. "There's something wrong with his little heart?"

"The two main arteries that leave his heart are switched," Peter explained. "This causes his body to be deprived of oxygen. That's why his skin is blue. We tried using a medication to shunt oxygen-rich blood to his body, but it isn't working. He needs to undergo surgery as soon as possible."

Lisa's mother began to weep silent tears.

Peter turned to the doorway—where Alex was standing. Alex wore an even-more-sour expression than usual, probably because this surgery would certainly thwart his plans to escape from the hospital that evening to go to the Twenty Claws concert.

"Lisa, this is Doctor Alex," Peter said. "He's going to perform your son's surgery."

Suddenly, Lisa gasped. "I can't ... breathe."

"She's desating," the OR nurse reported, her tone revealing the gravity of her statement.

As the nurse placed the oxygen mask back over Lisa's face, Connor grabbed his stethoscope.

"Pressure's dropping," Cassie said, concerned.

Connor glanced up at the monitor. Lisa's blood pressure was dangerously low. "Bolus her with a liter of saline," he said to the nurse.

Before the nurse could do anything, Lisa's eyes rolled up toward her forehead. Her body stiffened and then began to twitch.

"She's seizing," Connor said. "I need suction and a—"

"Sats are falling," the nurse said.

Lisa's oxygen level was now only sixty-five percent. Just seconds ago it had been ninety-seven percent. The nurse increased the amount of oxygen flowing through the oxygen mask, but Lisa's oxygen level continued to fall. Connor pulled a resuscitation bag from the crash cart.

"She's bradying down," Cassie said, her eyes wide with alarm.

By the time Connor pressed his fingers to Lisa's neck to check for a pulse, there was no blood pulsing through her arteries. The heart monitor showed a flat line. Lisa's heart had stopped.

"Start chest compressions," Connor ordered.

As Cassie began pushing on Lisa's chest, Nurse Samantha and Nurse Mike rushed into the room.

Connor quickly told them what had happened, "Patient desated, dropped her pressure, seized, and then went into full arrest. " Then he said, "Give her an amp of epi."

"What's happening?" Lisa's mother asked, her voice shaking.

Everyone was too busy trying to save Lisa to answer her—everyone except Alex.

Alex didn't look sour anymore. He walked over to Lisa's mother, put his hand on her shoulder, and explained, in a soft, gentle voice, "Lisa has stopped breathing and her heart has stopped beating. The doctors and nurses are pumping her heart, using a resuscitation bag to breathe for her, and giving her medications to try to get her heart started again."

"I'm going to intubate," Connor told his team. He needed to get Lisa's oxygen level up, and fast.

Nurse Mike took over the resuscitation bag. Connor slid a scope into Lisa's mouth and peered inside. Pink, frothy material filled Lisa's throat, obscuring Connor's view of her vocal cords. "She's got pulmonary edema," he said to his team. "I need suction!"

"Sats are falling," Nurse Samantha warned Connor.

Even though he could barely see Lisa's vocal cords, Connor slid the breathing tube deep into Lisa's throat. Mike attached the resuscitation bag to the end of the tube and squeezed air into Lisa's lungs. Her oxygen level came up a bit, but it was still only eighty percent—not even close to normal.

Samantha listened to Lisa's chest. "Breath sounds are equal, but with diffuse crackles."

"Why does she have pulmonary edema?" Connor asked himself out loud.

"It could be an amniotic fluid embolism," Cassie answered.

Connor had never seen a patient with an amniotic

fluid embolism, but he remembered learning about the condition. It is very rare and difficult to treat. Doctors don't know for sure what causes it or how to prevent it. It is thought that the condition is caused by the baby's amniotic fluid entering their mother's bloodstream, causing the mother's body to shut down. Unfortunately, patients with amniotic fluid embolism can die rapidly, despite everything doctors do to try to save them.

Cassie couldn't possibly be certain of that diagnosis, but the uncomfortable twisting in Connor's gut told him that Cassie might be right.

Chapter Ten

Trauma Room Three was filled with medical students, doctors, and nurses. Among them were Connor, Cassie, Brandon, Hannah, Connor's supervising ER doctor, Cassie's supervising obstetrician doctor, Nurse Samantha, and Nurse Mike. Brandon squeezed Lisa's resuscitation bag every few seconds. Cassie pushed on Lisa's chest to pump her heart. Alex had gone upstairs about thirty minutes ago to perform surgery on Lisa's baby.

Lisa's mother was seated on one side of the room next to an ER social worker—who had special training to support family members as they watch doctors and nurses try to save their loved ones.

Lisa didn't look like the same girl who had arrived in the ER a few hours ago. Now she lay flat on the ER table. A breathing tube was secured to one side of her upper lip like a grotesque pipe. A bit of blood stained each corner of her mouth. Wires were attached to her chest. IV lines punctured her body. Blood oozed from every puncture site.

Even though Connor was Lisa's doctor, all of the doctors and nurses in the room had been involved in caring for her. Together, they had decided which tests to order and interpreted the results of each test. Together, they had discussed every possible treatment to try. The doctors were now fairly certain that Lisa had experienced an amniotic fluid embolism, but despite everything they'd done to treat her over the past hour, Lisa's heart refused to beat.

Connor's supervising ER doctor, Doctor Dorothy, leaned close to Connor. "It's time to stop," she said.

Up until that point, Connor's mind had been occupied with ordering tests and blood products and medications, interpreting test results, and considering possible treatments. He hadn't considered giving up. But now Doctor Dorothy felt that it was time to terminate their efforts to save Lisa and to formally declare her dead. She felt that they had tried every reasonable intervention and that there was no significant chance that Lisa would recover if they were to continue.

Connor's body felt numb. He turned to his team and asked the final question that is asked of the medical team before any patient is declared dead at

Westley Hospital, "Does anyone have anything else that they think we should try before we stop?"

Connor waited, hopeful that someone would have a suggestion. But the room was silent except for the beeping of medical equipment. There was nothing more to do for Lisa.

"Okay then," Connor said.

He stepped away from the doctors and nurses, and he joined Lisa's tearful mother. Connor pulled up a stool, sat down next to her, and began, "As you know, about an hour ago, Lisa's heart stopped beating. Our medical team has tried everything they could to get it started again, but Lisa has not responded our interventions. We feel that, no matter what further steps we take, she will not recover. It's time for us to stop CPR. Would you like to say goodbye to Lisa before we do?"

Lisa's mother nodded stoically. Without displaying any emotion, she stood up and walked over to Lisa's gurney. She touched Lisa's forehead.

"Lisa?" she asked as if she thought Lisa might respond. But of course, Lisa didn't.

Cassie continued pushing on Lisa's chest to pump her heart. Brandon squeezed the resuscitation bag every few seconds to breathe for her.

Lisa's mother leaned in close to her daughter's ear. "I know I said I was disappointed in you. I want you to know that … I was wrong … I'm not … I'm not disappointed in you. I never really was. I was just upset. I love you, my baby girl. I always will. No matter what."

Lisa's mother wrapped her arms around her daughter's chest and let out a sob that echoed against the trauma room walls. Cassie could no longer pump Lisa's heart. Lisa's mother was in the way. Cassie looked up at Connor. Connor looked to Doctor Dorothy. Doctor Dorothy nodded.

"Time of death, seventeen twenty-seven," Connor said softly.

Cassie stepped away from Lisa's bed. Brandon disconnected Lisa's breathing tube from the resuscitation bag. Connor stared at Lisa's lifeless body. He wanted to scream in frustration, but instead he shoved his feelings as far down inside him as they would go and he turned and left the room.

Connor marched straight to the elevators, his eyes burning. He stepped into an empty elevator and pushed the button for the fourth floor. He wiped his eyes on the back of his fist, as the elevator doors opened.

Inside the OR prep room, Connor pulled on a bunny suit, a hat, shoe covers, and a mask, then he stepped out into the calm, quiet OR hallway. He checked the OR schedule and then made his way to OR Six. Silently, he slipped inside.

Alex's hands, holding skinny steel surgical instruments, danced above a very tiny chest. The heart was motionless. Thin hoses filled with the patient's blood snaked through the humming bypass machine.

Alex snipped a practically invisible thread with tiny scissors and said, without looking up, "Can someone call the ER? I want an update on the baby's mother."

"She's dead," Connor said, tears coming to his eyes.

Alex looked up at Connor, but he didn't say a word, then he looked back at his patient.

"Charge the paddles." Alex snatched the internal defibrillator paddles from a nurse and slid the ends into the baby's chest, cupping the heart between them.

"Clear," Alex commanded, and he pressed the red button on the grip of one of the paddles, jolting the heart with a burst of electricity.

The baby's heart quivered, but didn't start beating like it was supposed to.

"Give him epi," Alex said to the anesthesiologist. "Charge again." Alex placed the paddles back inside the baby's chest. "Come on, kid," he said under his breath.

"Epi's in," the anesthesiologist said.

"Clear!" Alex shocked the heart again.

The little heart just quivered feebly.

"Shoot," Alex said. He passed the paddles back to the nurse, reached into the baby's chest with both hands, and began massaging the heart.

Even though things were going horribly wrong, Alex seemed to be completely in control. Experienced doctors have an incredible ability to stay calm, even when things are falling apart around them. Connor wondered whether they ever feel helpless, the way he did that afternoon in Trauma Room Three.

Connor sensed someone, dressed in white, standing by his side. A warm hand touched his cool one. Connor turned to see Cassie, wearing a bunny suit.

"Are you okay?" Cassie whispered.

Suddenly, Alex barked, "Anyone who doesn't

need to be in here, get out!"

Connor and Cassie quickly turned and rushed out of the OR.

As soon as the door closed behind them, Connor turned to Cassie. "Follow me."

He opened a narrow door nearby and led Cassie up some steps and into a small observation room. Through the large window, they could see Alex working on Lisa's baby. The other side of the window looked like a mirror, so no one in the OR would know they were there.

Connor sat on one of the small yellow plastic chairs lined up along the window. Cassie sat next to him, and they both stared into the OR.

"I'm sorry I got you in trouble with your brother," Cassie said.

"He wasn't mad. He just likes to yell sometimes," Connor said.

Cassie exhaled. "How's Lisa's baby?"

"They put him on bypass and stopped his heart so Alex could repair it. Now they can't get it beating again," Connor said.

"Do you think he's going to survive?" Cassie asked.

"Alex will find a way to save him," Connor said confidently.

"Sometimes there's nothing that can be done, like with Lisa. My attending said we did everything right. She just got too sick too fast. I guess that happens a lot in the ER."

Connor shook his head. "I've never lost a patient … before today."

"I thought that people die all the time in the ER."

"Not at Westley Hospital," Connor said. "Have *you* ever lost a patient?"

"Two. At the same time. The mother's uterus ruptured. Both she and the baby died." She swallowed hard and then continued, her voice weak, "When your patients die, I think little pieces of you die too."

"What happens when you run out of pieces?" Connor asked.

"I don't know."

They sat quietly for a while. Finally, Connor said, "I saw you on the roof today. I'm surprised you went up there alone."

"I needed a good place to think."

"What were you thinking about?"

Cassie looked into his eyes. "If I have cancer, will

you still be my ... friend?"

"Are you kidding?" Connor covered her trembling hand with his. "Cassie, there isn't any diagnosis in the whole world that can make us not be friends anymore. Whatever *you* have, *we* have."

Tears sprung to Cassie's eyes, and she hugged Connor so tightly that he could feel her heart pounding in her chest. And then she pulled away. "What's in your pocket?" she asked, pressing her hand to the left side of his chest, where his own heart was now pounding.

Connor unzipped his bunny suit. He reached into his shirt pocket and pulled out the blood drawing supplies that he'd put there early that morning.

"Do you always carry that stuff around with you?" Cassie asked.

"I was hoping you'd change your mind about having those blood tests."

Cassie stared into the OR—where Alex was massaging Lisa's baby's heart. "I'm scared," she said, her voice shaky.

"Me too," Connor admitted. "But we need to make a diagnosis."

"I know," Cassie said. And then she unzipped her

bunny suit and presented her right arm to Connor. "Go ahead."

"You should probably lie down. Just in case …" Connor recalled the last time he'd drawn blood from Cassie.

Without arguing, Cassie reclined across the row of seats.

As Connor drew some of Cassie's blood into small glass tubes, Alex placed defibrillator paddles back into Lisa's baby's chest. A moment later, the little heart began to contract. Rhythmically. Perfectly.

"The baby's alive," Cassie breathed.

"I knew Alex would save him," Connor said. But as he looked at the tiny beating heart, he could only think of one thing: the fact that this baby's mother was dead.

Chapter Eleven

Connor and Cassie had just dropped off the vials of Cassie's blood at the lab when Connor's phone rang. On the caller ID was Alex's name.

Connor answered the phone. "Hi, Alex."

"You're late." Alex sounded annoyed.

"Late for what?" Connor asked.

"Our *meeting*."

It sounded like Alex was still planning to go to the Twenty Claws concert. Connor had thought that, with all that had happened that evening, their plans had been cancelled.

Connor swallowed. "We'll be right there."

"We're still going?" Cassie asked as Connor hung up the phone.

"I guess so," Connor said.

The two of them headed into the nearest stairwell and ran upstairs.

When they arrived at Alex's office, Connor gave a special knock, one that Alex and Connor had used on each other's doors back when they were little kids.

One of Alex's friends—Chris—cracked open the door and peered at them. Then he opened it enough for Connor and Cassie to enter.

A pile of severed security bands was on the floor of Alex's open closet.

"Here are your clothes," Alex said, tossing Connor and Cassie the bags of regular clothes they had hidden in his office in preparation for their escape. "Change in the closet," he ordered.

"You can go first," Connor said to Cassie.

"We don't have time for that," Alex snapped. "Just go together."

Connor knew better than to argue with Alex right now. He followed Cassie into the closet.

Alex slammed the door behind them and shouted, "Get a move on!"

"Sorry, Cassie," Connor whispered. "I won't look at—"

"It's no big deal," she said, turning on the light. "You've seen plenty of people's naked bodies." Cassie began to pull off her scrub top. Connor turned away.

"It's different with you," Connor said as he slid out of his scrub pants.

"Different how?" she asked.

He quickly slipped his jeans on and yanked off his scrub shirt. "I just ..."

Cassie touched his arm. Connor hastily put on the Twenty Claws t-shirt that his brother had given him and turned around. Cassie was now dressed in a flowing peach sundress. Her hair rested against her bare shoulders. Her eyes sparkled. She was more beautiful than anyone he had ever seen. Connor never wanted to kiss a girl as much as he wanted to kiss *this* girl.

"I like you," Connor said softly.

Cassie smiled the warmest smile ever. "I like you too."

"Time's up!" Alex banged the door open. "Get over here," he said to Connor.

Connor sat on the floor and lifted the right leg of his jeans, exposing his security band. He nervously watched as Alex placed the band between the Osteocisor's long, sharp blades. With one quick slice, the band fell away from Connor's ankle. He picked it up and examined it. On the inside was inscribed:

C. Hansen

Property of Westley Hospital

Connor threw his band into the closet with the others. Cassie's band joined it.

"Let's go," Alex said as he locked the Osteoscisor inside a cabinet. "Two at a time."

They left Alex's office in pairs. There were cameras everywhere, and they didn't want to arouse suspicion by leaving as a big group. Connor and Cassie stayed together and kept a close eye on Alex and Chris who were just in front of them. Connor was sure that Alex had discussed the details of the plan with everyone before they left, but Connor and Cassie had missed the briefing.

Alex and Chris led them to the third floor, where a walkway connected the hospital to a medical office building. Instead of heading into the office building, Alex climbed right over the side of the three-story-high walkway, and then disappeared from view, followed by Chris.

"What are they doing?" Cassie asked, her eyes wide with fear.

Connor leaned over the railing. Below, he saw Alex making his way down a rope ladder that was secured to the walkway's underside. Cassie peered over the wall as Alex landed on the ground with a hard thump.

Connor turned to Cassie. "Your platelets are low. You probably shouldn't—"

Cassie walked toward the ladder. "I'll be careful."

"I'll go first," Connor said.

Connor climbed over the wall and started down the ladder. When he looked up, he saw Cassie tentatively sliding her feet onto the top rungs. Connor began to descend slowly, steadily. Cassie followed his lead. When he stopped, she stopped. It was as if they were tethered together, climbing as just one person.

At the bottom of the ladder, Connor jumped off, landing on the grass below. Cassie continued down the final few rungs, then Connor reached up, put his hands on her waist, and eased her to the ground.

She stared into his eyes, her face just inches from his. "That was kinda fun."

Connor's heart pounded. He was pretty sure that Cassie wanted to kiss him. And he wanted to kiss her more than anything. If he could just work up the courage to—

"Out of the way!" Alex's friends Noah and Paul were just above them.

Connor and Cassie moved out from below the ladder. Connor tried to make eye contact with Cassie again, but she just stared at the ground.

They'd lost sight of Alex and Chris, and so they waited for Noah and Paul to jump down. Then they followed the older boys into the darkness.

* * *

Once they were safely out of sight of Westley Hospital, Alex and his friends regrouped. Everyone was buzzing with unrestrained excitement.

"Isn't this great, little bro?" Alex asked Connor. It had been a long time since Alex had called Connor his "little bro." Connor missed that time.

"It's *amazing*!" Connor beamed.

Alex broke into a run. Connor and Cassie followed, talking and laughing. They ran all the way to the Maren Stadium parking lot, which was completely packed with cars. As they neared the stadium entrance, Connor smelled something wonderful. Saliva pooled in his mouth. He hadn't eaten dinner yet, and now he suddenly felt ravenous.

"What is that awesome smell?" Connor called to Alex.

Alex stopped to read a sign above the only booth that hadn't already been shuttered for the evening. "Hot dogs."

A teen girl was inside the booth, packing up her supplies. "Want one?" she asked Alex.

"Sure," Alex said, staring at her, his jaw gaping open.

"How about you two?" the girl asked Cassie and Connor.

"Yes!" they answered.

"What do you want on yours?" the girl asked Alex as she used silver tongs to pull a perfectly-crispy-looking hot dog from the grill and drop it into a skinny bun.

"I've actually never had a hot dog before," Alex admitted.

The girl looked at him as if he'd told her he'd arrived at the stadium on a spaceship, then she smiled. "Then you should have the works."

"Okay," Alex agreed, even though he almost certainly didn't know what that meant.

"You guys want the works too?" she asked Connor and Cassie.

They nodded.

The girl lined up three hot dogs and topped them with a bunch of different toppings. Just when Connor thought she was done, she'd add another. Finally, she handed the hot dogs to their new owners.

"They look amazing," Alex said. "How much do I owe you?"

"They're on the house," she said. She reached into the refrigerator, pulled out three bottles of grape soda, and passed them out. "To wash them down."

"Thanks," Alex said, looking into the girl's eyes. Connor had never seen Alex look at anyone that way before.

"You're welcome," the girl breathed.

Alex smiled broadly at her and then turned awkwardly and headed toward the stadium. Cassie and Connor followed him.

Feeling bold, Connor asked Alex, "Do you *like* her?"

"I guess," Alex said, as he took a big bite of his hot dog.

Connor glanced back toward the hot dog stand. The girl was watching them.

"He likes you," Connor mouthed to the girl.

"I like him too," she mouthed back.

Connor turned to share that news with Alex, but Alex was already at the turnstiles, entering the stadium. As Connor and Cassie ran to catch up, Connor's pager beeped. He grabbed it and checked the number. His giddy excitement instantly changed to gut-twisting anxiety.

"It's the lab," he told Cassie.

They both knew what this meant: Cassie's lab results were ready.

"I should call them," Connor said.

"Yeah," Cassie agreed.

As Connor pulled out his phone and dialed, a horrible screeching sound came from the parking lot. A car was barreling toward them, brakes squealing. Connor grabbed Cassie's arm and yanked her of the way. As they fell to the sidewalk, Cassie on top of Connor, the car whizzed past them and slammed into the base of a huge signpost. The front end of the car soared into the air and the back end spun in a circle, leveling everything in its path, including the little hot dog stand.

Deadly silence was interrupted by the sound of a distant announcer. "And now ... Twenty Claws!"

The crowd inside the stadium cheered ecstatically.

Music began to play.

Connor and Cassie helped each other to their feet.

"You okay?" Connor asked her.

"Yeah," she said. "You?"

"Yeah," Connor said. And then he looked at the ruined hot dog stand. "Call 911!" he said to Cassie, and then he turned and ran toward the wreckage.

Connor climbed up a shaky tower of broken cement—all the way up to the car's broken passenger window. When he looked inside, he knew instantly that there was nothing anyone could do to help this man. Connor had seen many seriously injured patients, but he had never seen anything this horrible. Patients like this don't come to the hospital. They go straight to the morgue. Connor shivered.

"The ambulance is on its way," Cassie called up to Connor.

"The driver's dead," Connor called down. "Wait there. I'm going to go look for that girl."

Connor climbed down from the pile of cement and ventured into what was once the hot dog stand. He understood that what he might find there could be even more terrible than what he had just seen.

"Hello?" Connor shouted into the dust, hoping for

an answer but not expecting one.

And then, he heard a very weak voice say, "Help!"

Below some large shards of metal and broken glass, Connor found the girl who had just served them hot dogs, lying on the ground. Her skin was covered in bloody scrapes and scratches, but otherwise, she looked okay.

"Cassie, I found her!" Connor shouted.

The girl started to get up.

"Lie still," Connor instructed the girl. "You're not supposed to move." He pressed his fingers against the side of the girl's neck. Her pulse was weak.

"You're a Boy Scout?" she asked, a smile forming on her lips.

"I'm a doctor."

The girl's forehead creased with confusion. "Are you serious?"

Cassie poked her head out from under some torn plastic. "The EMTs are here!"

"Is he ... really a doctor?" the girl asked Cassie.

"Yeah," Cassie said. "That guy who was with us is too."

"That's so ... cool ... I want ... to be a doctor ...

someday ..." the girl said, breathlessly. Connor wished he could give her some oxygen.

A man and a woman wearing Emergency Medical Technician uniforms pushed through the rubble. "Stand back, kid. We're going to help your friend," the male EMT shouted out.

The girl winced. "My chest ... hurts ..." And then her face went lifeless.

The male EMT turned to his partner. "Poor respiratory effort. Bag her," he ordered.

Connor spotted a stethoscope in the EMTs' bag and grabbed it. He listened to the girl's chest. "Heart sounds are muffled," he reported.

"BP sixty over forty," the male EMT said to his partner.

Connor noticed that the veins on the girl's neck were now bulging unnaturally. He began putting the information together in his mind. *Muffled heart sounds ... low blood pressure ... bulging neck veins.* Connor made a diagnosis: pericardial tamponade. The sac around the girl's heart was filling with blood. The blood was squishing her heart so much that it wasn't able to pump. He needed to do something, now!

"We need to perform a pericardiocentesis,"

Connor said to the EMTs.

"What did you say?" the male EMT asked.

Connor slipped his hospital ID badge out from under his t-shirt. "I'm an emergency room doctor at Westley Hospital—"

"I didn't think they let you kids out and about," the EMT said.

"They don't," Connor responded. "I need a pericardiocentesis needle."

"We don't carry those," the EMT said. "We've called for ALS back up. They should be here soon."

"This girl's got pericardial tamponade. Her heart's hardly pumping. In five minutes, she'll be brain dead. I need antiseptic and sterile gloves."

The man reached into his bag and then tossed Connor a package of sterile gloves.

"Gloves for her too," Connor said, nodding toward Cassie.

The man handed a second pack of gloves to Cassie, and he pulled out a small packet of brown liquid that is used to clean patients' skin before surgeries and other medical procedures.

"Pour that here," Connor said, pointing to the left side of the girl's chest.

The man doused the girl's chest in antiseptic.

"Scalpel!" Connor said, holding out his hand.

The EMTs just stared at him. Connor was fairly sure that they didn't think it was a good idea to give him a surgical knife.

"Scalpel!" Connor repeated, trying to sound strong and certain, trying to instill confidence in his team.

The man pulled a scalpel from his bag and opened the package, offering the razor-sharp knife to Connor. Connor took the scalpel and sliced into the girl's chest, cutting deeper and deeper. It was his first emergency thoracotomy. Although he had been trained to perform this procedure, he had been trained to do it in an emergency room stocked full of supplies, equipment, and highly trained ER doctors and nurses who were ready to offer assistance if necessary. Here, the only available equipment seemed to be a scalpel. And he was pretty sure that he was the only person here who had ever put their hands inside someone's chest. There was no one to guide him.

"Hold ventilations," Connor instructed the female EMT.

Connor carefully pierced the girl's chest cavity

with the scalpel and cautiously extended the cut up and down.

"Resume ventilations," Connor said. "Cassie, retract the ribs."

Cassie grabbed hold of the girl's ribs and pulled them apart, creating an opening in the girl's chest that was large enough for Connor to reach inside. Connor pushed the girl's floppy, pink lung out of his way with one hand, and used his other hand to feel for her heart.

"I wish I had more light," Connor said under his breath.

The male EMT pulled a flashlight from his belt and shined the light into the girl's open chest.

"Thanks," Connor said, and then he saw the pericardium. The sac around the heart was bulging, just as he had suspected. He sliced into it and blood poured out.

"What the heck are you—?" the male EMT started.

"How's her pulse?" Connor asked him.

The man placed his fingers on the girl's neck. "It's good," he said, his shoulders relaxing.

"Can you recheck her BP, please?" Connor asked the female EMT.

"Yeah, sure," she said, grabbing the stethoscope.

Someone pushed their way through the wreckage. "Connor ..." It was Alex.

Connor briefed Alex on his patient, the same way he would if they were in the ER, "Auto versus ped. She had pericardial tamponade, and she was crashing. The EMTs didn't have any pericardiocentesis needles, so I performed an open drainage. She needs to go to the OR for definitive repair—"

"BP's coming up," the female EMT said, smiling. "Ninety over sixty-two."

"Good job, little bro," Alex said.

Connor had never felt more proud.

Chapter Twelve

When Connor was a little, he had wanted to go for an ambulance ride, but his dad said it was too dangerous. Connor used to imagine what it would be like to sit in the front seat, with the ambulance lights and sirens going at full blast, as they raced through the city streets. He was finally getting his ambulance ride, but it wasn't at all like he'd imagined.

He and Alex sat side-by-side on a bench in the back of the ambulance, staring at their patient. A clear plastic oxygen mask covered her mouth and nose. The paramedics had placed a stiff plastic and foam collar around her neck and strapped her to a long plastic board to keep her spine immobile, in case her back had been injured in the accident. A blood pressure cuff, a finger sensor, and some wires attached to her chest were connected to a monitor.

At the moment, the girl's vital signs were stable. Connor hoped they stayed that way. Even though the ambulance had lots of medical equipment, it might not have everything they needed to save her if she started to die again.

Cassie rode up front with the driver. Connor was pretty sure Cassie wasn't enjoying the ambulance ride either.

"We're here," the driver said, backing up to Westley Hospital's emergency room entrance.

The ambulance's back doors popped open. Doctors and nurses with gloved hands reached into the ambulance and guided the gurney toward them. Connor and Alex jumped out into the cool night air.

Brandon stared at them, his jaw gaping. "Connor?" He sounded surprised, and a bit impressed.

Connor presented his patient to the ER team as they rushed her inside the building, "Teen female. Status post auto versus pedestrian. Pericardial tamponade status post open drainage. Vitals have been stable during transport."

Alex took over speaking, "I need to get her to the OR ASAP. Make sure there are no other significant injuries, and then send her up."

"Done," Adam—one of the Twelfth Year ER doctors—said.

The ER team whisked their patient into Trauma Room Two.

Standing outside the room was Mark.

"Dad!" Connor said.

"Connor. Alex." Mark spoke slowly and deliberately. Connor could tell that he was livid.

"I saved this girl's life, Dad," Connor said.

"You left hospital grounds without my knowledge. You could have been the ones who needed saving," Mark said.

"Dad, we're fine," Alex said dismissively. "Are we through here? I need to go get the OR ready for this patient."

"When you're done with the surgery, I want to see you in my office," Mark said.

Without acknowledging the instruction, Alex walked past him, headed to the elevators.

"Connor, come with me. We need to talk," Mark said.

Cassie raced around the corner and ran up to Connor. "How's she doing?" she asked.

Before Connor could answer, Mark spun toward him. "You took Cassie with you?" he asked in a low, angry voice.

"He didn't *take* me anywhere. I *wanted* to go," Cassie said.

"Go home, Cassie," Mark said.

Cassie exhaled. "Good night, Connor."

"Good night, Cassie."

Mark turned back to Connor. "My office, now!"

* * *

Connor sat uncomfortably, across from his dad, in his dad's perfectly arranged office. Numerous framed awards hung on the walls. Glossy, photo-filled magazine articles touting the success of the Kid Docs program and Westley Hospital were also proudly displayed. His dad's smiling face in the photos contrasted sharply with the face Connor saw in front of him.

"May I see your right ankle?" Mark asked, but he seemed to already know what he was about to find there.

Connor reluctantly lifted the leg of his jeans.

Mark glanced at Connor's ankle and then looked him in the eyes. "What happened to your security band?"

"It was cut off," Connor said.

"By whom?" Mark asked.

Connor didn't answer.

Mark exhaled. "*Why* was it cut off?"

"So I could go to a concert," Connor admitted. He was certain that his father already knew this.

"Twenty claws?" Mark asked. He seemed to already know this too.

Connor nodded.

"You don't like Twenty Claws," Mark said.

"I thought it would be fun to go anyway."

"Because Alex was going?" Mark asked. His tone was gentler now.

"Alex and I never do anything fun together anymore," Connor's voice trembled with frustration. "He's always so angry."

"Well, that's going to change. A lot of things around here are going to change."

Connor stiffened. "What do you mean?"

"Do you know why this is called *Westley* Hospital?"

Connor had never really thought about it. "I figured it was somebody's name."

"It *is* somebody's name. It's the name of our corporate sponsor."

"What's a corporate sponsor?"

"It's a business that gives us a lot of money to

keep this place running. Without them, we would be forced to shut down. Our corporate sponsor is Westley Security. They made those tracking bands you boys cut off. They're pretty embarrassed about that. The news media is having a field day with this: 'Teens Break Through Westley Security.' They're withdrawing their sponsorship."

"We can get a new corporate sponsor," Connor offered.

"It's not that easy, Connor," Mark said, and then he asked, "Do you know why I started the Kid Docs program?"

To Connor, that felt like a ridiculous question. He'd heard his dad tell the story of Kid Docs to so many reporters that he could recite that story himself: *In the beginning, it was just an idea. During my own medical training, it occurred to me that there was so much to know about medicine that, by the time a doctor reaches the point where their knowledge and experience make them a truly great doctor, their career is already half over. I thought if I could find those same individuals when they were very young, and have them live and breathe medicine, that they could become extraordinary doctors ... superdoctors.*

"To create superdoctors," Connor said aloud.

"That's what I tell the newspapers and magazines, but that's not the real reason," Mark said.

Connor felt his skin turn cold. "What's the real reason?"

"I started it for you and Alex. After your mother died, the two of you cried all of the time. But you would always stop crying was when I read to you from your mother's surgery books. The strange thing was, you actually seemed to understand what I was reading, even though you were just a baby. And Alex ... I think he understood more than some cardiothoracic surgery fellows. I thought being doctors would make you happy. Whatever it took, I wanted so badly to make you happy. I realize now that I failed. And for that, I'm sorry."

His head lowered, Mark got up and left the office.

Connor just sat there, staring at the wall of awards, feeling like his world was crumbling around him. And then, his pager beeped. Doctor Keith had sent him a text message:

Labs on your Jane Doe are back.
Please call to discuss.

* * *

When Connor woke up the next morning, even though he wasn't scheduled to work that day, he felt like he had a million things to do.

First, he had to talk to Cassie. He sent her a text message asking her to meet him on the hospital roof. He knew they would have some privacy there.

When Cassie opened the hatch to the roof, Connor was waiting. He led her to a small concrete box and sat on top of it.

"Have a seat," he said. He'd been taught that important news should always be given to people when they are sitting down.

Cassie sat next to him.

"I went over your latest labs with Doctor Keith," Connor began. "He feels that your diagnosis is mononucleosis."

"How do you treat that?" Cassie asked.

"You don't," Connor said. "It's a self-limited viral infection. It goes away on its own."

"So, I don't have cancer?" Cassie asked, her eyes hopeful.

"Doctor Keith would like to run some follow up labs on you next week, but at this point he's fairly confident that you do not have cancer."

Cassie's face lit up with a smile. Then she asked, "Am I contagious?"

"Possibly," Connor answered.

Cassie stared hard into Connor's eyes. "That sucks, because I really wish I could kiss you right now."

Without allowing himself even an instant to reconsider, Connor closed his eyes and leaned toward her. Cassie's lips were warm and soft, and they smelled like fresh strawberries. A wave of heat embraced him as they tentatively explored each other's mouths. In those moments, his world seemed to stop crumbling. Connor felt certain that everything was going to be all right.

When they finally separated, Cassie's cheeks were flushed almost as red as her hair. "That was so wonderful," she said, and then she turned toward the view, resting her head against his shoulder.

"It was," Connor said. He closed his eyes and took a slow, deep breath, trying to recover from that incredible first kiss. His first kiss ever.

* * *

As Connor and Cassie made their way from the roof to the stairwell, Cassie said, "My parents are going to let me adopt that kitten we found in the old PICU. Will you come with me to get him?"

Even though Connor still had a ton of things to do, he said, "Of course."

They stopped at the labor and delivery unit, where Cassie got an empty cardboard box from the nurses, then Connor and Cassie headed to the old PICU.

They found Cassie's kitten hiding in a long-abandoned PICU sink. Cassie lifted him into her arms. "Hey, PICU!"

"You're going to name him PICU?" Connor asked.

"Can you think of a better name?"

Connor could think of lots of better names, but this was Cassie's kitten, and so he just said, "PICU it is."

Suddenly, a door squeaked open. Cassie placed the kitten into her cardboard box and she and Connor dashed into the closet to hide.

"It's probably just a janitor," Connor whispered.

"Ghosty!" a girl called out.

Connor recognized the voice. It was Hannah. He froze.

"Ghosty?" Hannah called again.

The kitten pawed at the box, and Connor realized something: *Hannah has been taking care of the kitten.* Then Connor had an awful thought: what if that crash they'd heard on the night they'd snuck into the old PICU had been caused by Hannah. That would explain why she seemed so certain that Cassie was his girlfriend. If Hannah had seen them lying on top of the nurses' station desk, staring into each other's eyes, what else could she have thought?

The closet door opened, and Hannah peered inside. Her expression instantly fell. She looked as if she was going to vomit.

"Hannah, this is Cassie," Connor said, feeling sick to his stomach as well. "Cassie, this is Hannah." He wasn't sure what else to say.

Hannah pointed to the box in Cassie's arms. "What's in there?"

Cassie opened the box, and the little white kitten poked his head out.

"Ghosty!" Hannah took the kitten from the box,

snuggling him against her cheek, and then she turned back to Cassie. "Why did you put him in that box?"

"I'm going to adopt him," Cassie answered.

"You can't. He's mine," Hannah said. "I found him wandering around all alone outside the hospital."

"Why didn't you take him home?" Cassie asked.

"My mom has allergies," Hannah said. "We can't have any pets."

Cassie stood up next to Hannah, and gently stroked the fur behind the kitten's ears. "The hospital isn't a safe place for a kitten to live," she said. "He needs a home."

As if on cue, the kitten let out a plaintive, "Mew."

Hannah's eyes filled with tears. "You're right. He does."

"I'll take really good care of him," Cassie said. "And you can come visit him if you want."

Hannah held Cassie's gaze for a moment, and then she kissed the kitten on the forehead. Tenderly, she placed him into Cassie's box and closed the top. "Take him," Hannah said to Cassie.

Connor's mouth dropped open. It wasn't like Hannah to give in so easily. Maybe Hannah trusted Cassie because *he* trusted Cassie. Hannah trusted him, and he trusted her. They were best friends. But he hadn't acted like it recently. Connor felt a squeeze of regret in his stomach.

As they left the old PICU, he let Cassie walk ahead of him and Hannah.

"I'm sorry I said you and I weren't friends anymore," Connor said to Hannah. "Of course we're still friends ... if you want to be."

"Of course I want to be your friend, Connor." Hannah gave him a small smile, but her eyes held a hint of sadness.

Connor draped his arm over Hannah's shoulders, and she put her arm over his shoulders, the way they used to do when they were younger, back when people used to call them twins.

"Cassie *is* your girlfriend, isn't she?" Hannah asked softly.

Connor was finally certain of the answer. "Yes, she is."

Hannah sighed almost imperceptibly. "I like her. She seems nice."

Connor gave Hannah a squeeze. "She is."

Chapter Thirteen

On the ICU board—where all of the patients' names were listed—there was only one Jane Doe. She was in Room Four. Connor hoped she was the girl from the stadium. If she wasn't, it would mean that the girl from the stadium hadn't survived the night.

Connor hesitantly looked through the sliding glass door of Room Four. He didn't breathe until he saw that the girl in the bed was the same girl whose chest he'd cut open the evening before. She was still alive. Next to her, asleep in a chair, was Alex.

Connor quietly slid the door open and entered the room. He stood near the bed, watching the girl breathe, not quite believing that, less than twenty-four hours ago, the same girl was dying in a pile of rubble. He and Alex had saved her life.

The girl slowly opened her eyes. Connor looked away, trying to pretend he hadn't been staring at her.

"You were in my dream," the girl whispered hoarsely.

Alex startled awake and sat up in his chair.

The girl looked at Alex and smiled. "So were you." Suddenly, her smile vanished, replaced by an expression of pure panic. She reached to the left side of her chest, where her fingers found a plastic tube filled with bloody fluid sticking out of her ribcage. "What happened to me?"

Alex put his hand on her arm. "You were hit by a car. But you're safe now. You're at the hospital."

"What did they do to me?" she asked, touching the thick gauze taped to her chest, over her heart.

"After the accident, blood accumulated in the sac around your heart," Alex said. He nodded toward Connor and continued, "Connor drained the blood from the sac to keep you alive, and then I took you to the OR to repair the torn—"

"You're doctors?" The girl looked from Connor to Alex and back again.

"Yeah," they said.

The girl looked at Alex, as if his image stirred up memories from deep in her mind. "I gave you a hot dog and a soda ... for free, because you were cute."

Alex looked at his shoes, his cheeks turning red.

The girl looked at Connor. "Your name's Connor?"

Connor nodded.

"Nice to meet you, Connor," she said, shaking Connor's hand.

Then she looked at Alex. "And what's your name?"

"Alex ... Alex Hansen," Alex stammered.

Erica offered her hand to him. "I'm Erica Maren."

"Erica *Maren*?" Connor asked. "As in *Maren* Stadium?"

"My dad's company sponsors the stadium, among other things," Erica answered, without looking away from Alex.

Connor hated to ask, but he was desperate. "You think he'd be interested in sponsoring a hospital?"

* * *

Connor sprinted down the hall, into the stairwell, up the stairs, out of the stairwell, down another hall, and straight into his father's office.

"Dad, guess what?" Connor shouted, gasping for air.

Mark was standing and staring at a television. "I already know."

Connor followed his dad's gaze to the television.

On the news, a reporter was standing in front of Westley Hospital. Behind her were many of his fellow Kid Docs, holding signs.

One sign declared:

No rock concerts!
No fair!

The reporter was saying, "… the child doctors are threatening to continue to strike until their demands are met, another crushing blow to the already-troubled Westley Hospital."

Mark sighed. "You seem to have inspired quite a number of your colleagues."

Connor shook his head. "We didn't tell them to do this."

As he spoke, the news camera panned over to show a very young Kid Doc who had written, in big letters, on his sign:

Connor and Alex are my heroes!

"You didn't have to," his dad said.

Connor spun around and ran out of his dad's

office, down the hallway, into the stairwell, down the stairs, out of the stairwell, through the hospital lobby, and into the chaotic courtyard. As he ran, he managed to send a message to Cassie:

Big problem! Turn on the news.

As Connor made his way into the courtyard crowd, some of the other Kid Docs spotted him and started chanting his name.

Someone handed him a megaphone. Connor pushed the button and spoke into it uncertainly, "Thank you for your support."

The other Kid Docs yelled words of encouragement, waving their signs above their heads.

Connor continued, "I guess most of you believe that some of the rules here just aren't right. And if rules aren't right, we shouldn't have to follow them."

There were excited murmurs from the crowd. Everyone seemed to agree with what he was saying.

Connor kept speaking, "For years, we've followed the rules without questioning them. That needs to change."

The murmurs grew even louder.

Connor went on, "But this is not how to change things."

The crowd fell silent.

Connor took a breath before he started again, "If things are broken, they need to be assessed and repaired, not recklessly abandoned." Cassie appeared in the crowd as Connor kept going, "As a doctor, I should have realized that. But I made a mistake. Last night, a group of your colleagues and I acted irresponsibly. As a direct result of our actions, the hospital has lost the sponsorship of Westley Security. If we are unable to find a new sponsor, the hospital will be shut down. How many of you would like to leave this place behind?"

The crowd remained quiet.

Connor swallowed away the lump in his throat. "That's what I thought."

Alex moved through the crowd along with a gray-haired man in a dark business suit. Connor didn't recognize the man. He wondered whether the hospital had hired a new publicist to deal with this public relations nightmare.

The man offered his hand to Connor. "Doctor Connor, it is a true pleasure to meet you."

Connor was puzzled. The man hadn't introduced himself. Connor looked to Alex for a clue.

"This is Erica's dad, Mr. Maren," Alex said.

Mr. Maren looked at the megaphone. "May I?"

Alex nodded encouragingly to Connor, and Connor handed over the megaphone.

"For those of you who don't know me, my name is Anthony Maren." Mr. Maren's booming voice echoed through the courtyard. "My daughter is a patient at this hospital. She is alive as a direct result of the care provided by the doctors, nurses, and hospital staff who work here. There is no way I can ever repay what you have done, but I'm going to try. One thing I've learned in business is that it's difficult to work hard if you're not happy. I'd like to see what I can do to make you ecstatic." Mr. Maren looked at one of the Kid Doc's signs. "You want to go to a rock concert? I know a great stadium."

Some of the older Kid Docs hooted ecstatically.

"Maybe we can also set something up right here on the hospital lawn," Mr. Maren added.

Thrilled hoots followed that idea.

"But that's not all. I would like to make this the most state-of-the-art hospital in the world. What do you say? Would any of you like to work at *Maren* Hospital?"

The Kid Docs roared in approval.

"Then get in there and show the world what we can do!" Connor shouted.

The Kid Docs whooped and cheered as they headed back into the hospital.

Connor turned and found himself face-to-face with his father.

"Dad!" Connor said. "This is Mr. Maren."

Mr. Maren shook Mark's hand and then he said, "Last night your sons took care of my daughter. I understand that the hospital is in a bit of financial trouble, and I'd like to help. I'm interested in taking over sponsorship. I'd like to make this Maren Hospital."

"That's extremely generous. Thank you," Mark said, and then he turned and walked away.

Connor and Alex caught up to their father. "Dad, where are you going?" Connor asked.

"The doctors are back to work. The hospital has a potential new sponsor. Everything seems to be under control."

"Then why are you upset?" Connor asked.

"Because it's time for me to step down."

"'Step down'?" Connor repeated, puzzled.

"I think that would be best, after all that's happened. Someone needs to take the blame." He put his hand on Alex's shoulder. "And you don't have to be a doctor anymore." He looked at Connor. "Neither do you, Connor. From now on, I'll do my best to give the two of you a normal life. No hospitals. No surgeries—"

"But I like being a doctor," Alex said.

"It's okay, Alex, you don't have to pretend for my sake," Mark said.

"I'm not pretending," Alex insisted. "It used to be that I liked surgery because it was a challenge. Then it got easy and it stopped being fun. But I realized something last night. The reason I take people to the OR ... the reason I fix their hearts is for what's *inside their hearts*."

Mark looked into Alex's eyes, as if he were seeing something he never had before.

"What?" Alex asked.

Mark smiled. "You just ... reminded me of your mother."

Alex gave his dad a huge hug. He reached out and

pulled Connor into the hug too. Cassie stood a few feet away, watching them and smiling. Connor smiled back at her. He hadn't felt this happy in a very long time. And he had a feeling that, this time, his happiness was going to last.

* * *

Outside the neonatal intensive care unit, Connor, Cassie, and Alex washed their hands and pulled yellow gowns over their clothes—in order to minimize the germs entering the area where the tiniest patients in the hospital are cared for.

They walked past rows of baby warmers, where fragile-looking babies were fighting for their lives. Most of the babies were unbelievably small. They had been born too early. Connor saw one baby who was only about the size of an adult's hand.

On one of the warmers was Lisa's baby. A gauze pad covered the surgical wound on his chest. Skinny tubes sprung from his belly button and wires connected him to monitors. Still, he didn't look nearly as sick as the other babies on the warmers. Lisa's baby was awake and very alert. He stared intensely into the eyes of a boy who looked about the same age as Alex.

The baby's little fist tightly held onto the boy's finger.

Lisa's mother spotted Connor, Cassie and Alex. She lifted her gaze to them and spoke quietly, "Doctors, this is David, Lisa's boyfriend ... her baby's father." Then she turned to David. "Doctor Connor and Doctor Cassie delivered your baby and took care of Lisa. Doctor Alex fixed your little boy's heart."

"Hi," David said, his eyes remaining focused on the baby.

"How was the heart ultrasound?" Lisa's mother asked, her eyes worried.

"Everything looked good," Alex told her. "He'll need close follow-up, but I expect him to do very well."

"How are *you* doing?" Cassie asked Lisa's mother.

"I'm having a hard time," she responded, tears pooling in her eyes.

An overwhelming ache squeezed Connor's chest. All of the helplessness that he'd felt yesterday in Trauma Room Three suddenly came flooding back to him, making his head dizzy.

Tomorrow, he would have to go back to work in the ER.

How would he be able to do that?

* * *

Alex had gone to the ICU to see Erica Maren, and so Cassie and Connor stepped into the empty elevator alone. Cassie pushed the button for the lobby, and then she turned to Connor. "You okay?" she asked.

"When your patient dies, how do you go on as if nothing has happened?" Connor asked.

Cassie's eyes flashed with understanding. "You don't," she said. "You just *go on*. You take care of the next—"

Connor's pager beeped. He checked it and then took a breath. "The ICU is paging me." He wasn't sure why.

"Do you want me to come with you?" she asked.

"No, I'll text you when I'm done."

"Okay," Cassie said.

The elevator let Cassie off in the lobby and then Connor took it back upstairs. As he entered the ICU, Doctor Robin waved him over. Doctor Keith was sitting next to him at the nurses' station.

"Did you page me?" Connor asked Robin.

"You asked to be called when oncology came by

regarding Mr. North," Robin said.

"Right," Connor said. He turned to Keith. "What do you think of the pulmonary lesion?"

"The mass looks suspicious," Keith said. "But based on the pattern of calcification, I'd be willing to bet that it isn't malignant. Of course we'll need to do some studies to confirm that, especially given his smoking history."

"Have you talked to him yet?" Connor asked.

"No, I'm going in now," Keith said.

"Is it okay if I join you," Connor asked.

Keith nodded, and he, Connor, and Robin walked to ICU Room Seven.

Mr. North was on the phone when they arrived at his door. His son, Aaron, was lounging in a chair reading from a thick textbook.

"The doctors are here. I'll have to call you later," Mr. North said into the phone.

"We can come back," Keith offered.

"Nonsense. Come on in. I need to know when I'm getting out of here," Mr. North said.

"I should be able to transfer you to the telemetry unit within a day or so," Robin said, "but there's something else we need to discuss."

Keith looked at Aaron and then back to Mr. North. "It would be best if we speak with you privately."

Aaron stood up. "I'll be in the waiting room."

After Aaron stepped out, Doctor Keith introduced himself to Mr. North, "I'm Doctor Keith, from oncology."

Mr. North's forehead creased.

"Back when you were in the emergency room, they did a chest x-ray," Keith began. "On the x-ray, there was a concerning spot—"

"It's cancer isn't it?" Mr. North asked.

"We're not sure," Keith answered. "We'll need to do some additional studies."

"I figured my past would catch up with me one of these days," Mr. North said. "I've been smoking since I was sixteen. Aaron just took it up too. It kills me to see him do that, but I can't get either one of us to stop."

"We can help you," Connor offered.

"You'd be wasting your time. I've tried to quit ... again and again. But I keep going back."

Connor couldn't give up. "I made a promise on the day I became a doctor—"

"The Hippocratic Oath, I know," Mr. North said.

"I was talking about a different promise ... a promise I made to my dad," Connor said. "He told me that, whenever I ask a patient to do something important, I need to them *why* they should do it. But not just the medical reason. The personal reason. Of course, most of the time, doctors don't know their patients well enough to know their personal reason. And so he gave me a story to tell to help them figure it out. I'd like to tell that story to you if that's okay."

Mr. North sighed, but he didn't ask him to stop, and so Connor continued, "It's about a woman who started smoking when she was in junior high. Everyone told her that she should quit, but she just couldn't give it up. Until she got pregnant with her first child. That's when she finally quit. She said that she wanted to see her child grow up. To see him get married. To be a grandma to his kids. She quit the day she found out she was pregnant. Her baby was her *why*. Unfortunately, her *why* had come too late. A few years later, she was still a nonsmoker and was pregnant with her second child when she was diagnosed with cancer. She refused treatment for the cancer, because chemotherapy would harm the baby developing inside her. She died a few weeks after her baby was born."

Mr. North cleared his throat. "Is that a true story?"

Connor nodded, feeling as if he might cry. "It's my mom's story."

"I'm so sorry." Mr. North put a gentle hand on Connor's shoulder, and he swallowed hard. "Would you mind ... at some point ... telling that story to my son? I think it might help."

Connor went to the waiting room and led Aaron back to ICU. And then he told him the same story he'd told Mr. North. The story Connor had known for as long as he could remember.

The story about his mother.

Chapter Fourteen

Connor burst into the sunshine. Rock music filled the air, along with the excited chatter and delighted squeals of people enjoying the carnival that had been set up on the hospital lawn. Connor eyed the gigantic Ferris wheel. He couldn't wait to ride it!

He was about to text Cassie when he heard a man's voice call out, "Doctor Connor!"

Connor spun around to see Mr. Peterson in a wheelchair. He looked much stronger and healthier than he did when Connor had last seen him, over a month ago. Mr. Peterson's wife was standing next to him. She held the hand of a little girl—who looked like she was about six years old—and carried a baby boy in her arms.

"You remember my wife, Lucy," Mr. Peterson said to Connor. "And this is my son, Trevor, and my daughter, Olivia. Olivia drew those pictures that I gave you."

Connor turned to Olivia. "Those pictures are awesome! Thank you so much!"

Olivia shyly buried her face in her mother's dress.

"I have to get going," Mr. Peterson said. "I'm starting physical therapy today. I don't want to be late for my appointment." He turned to Olivia. "Mommy is going to take you to the carnival while I do my exercises."

As Mr. Peterson kissed his daughter, wife, and son, his eyes filled with tears. After Olivia bounced away, followed by her mother, Mr. Peterson nodded at Connor appreciatively. "Thank you again, Doctor Connor ... for *everything*." Then he rolled off.

Connor texted Cassie to find out where she was, and then he walked toward the concert stage where Twenty Claws was performing for an enthusiastic audience of doctors, hospital staff, and patients. Close to the stage, a group of young patients danced to the music. Connor recognized one of the little boys. Even though a surgical mask covered most of his face—to protect him from germs—and his curly blond hair had been shed due to the medicines that were treating his illness, Connor could tell that it was Timothy. A little girl who wore a pink hat over her bald head took Timothy's hand. He twirled under her arm.

Connor spotted Erica Maren and Alex sitting

close together on the stairs at the edge of the stage. Over the past few weeks, Alex and Erica had become close friends. Alex had become much more pleasant too. He hardly ever yelled anymore.

Connor felt a warm hand slide into his. It was Cassie's.

"Well, we finally got to go to a Twenty Claws concert," she said above the noise of the band. She gave an apologetic smile. "I'm not really a fan of their music."

Connor smiled back. "Me neither."

The song mercifully ended, the audience applauded loudly, and Twenty Claws left the stage.

Mark stepped up to the microphone. "Thank you, Twenty Claws!" he said politely. Then he turned to the crowd. "We are gathered here today to recognize a man who has made a monumental contribution to this hospital. I'd like to present to you: Mr. Anthony Maren."

As Mr. Maren approached the microphone, people hooted and applauded, even louder as they did for Twenty Claws.

"Thank you, Doctor Hansen," Mr. Maren said, and then he turned to the crowd. "Up until two weeks ago, I had only read about this institution. A hospital with child doctors? Interesting idea, but I'd rather be treated by a *regular* doctor. Last week, I received a phone call. My daughter was a patient at 'the kid hospital.' I jumped into my car expecting the worst, but what I found were some of the most caring, talented physicians I have ever met. They saved my child's life. When I heard that the hospital was in financial trouble, I decided to take action. I wanted to make this *Maren* Hospital ... I have, however, changed my mind."

The crowd buzzed with concern, but Connor looked at Cassie and grinned knowingly.

"About the name, that is," Mr. Maren continued. "Doctor Hansen, if it's okay with you, I'd like to name this remarkable institution: Mark Hansen Hospital."

Mark's jaw dropped.

"What do you think?" Mr. Maren asked the audience.

"Doctor Mark ... Doctor Mark ..." Hannah chanted.

"Doctor Mark ... Doctor Mark ..." Cassie joined in.

Soon all of the Kid Docs were shouting out words

of support.

Mr. Maren gave a wave of his hand and the drape covering the new hospital sign was lifted, revealing shiny silver lettering that proclaimed:

Mark Hansen Hospital

Connor ran up to his father. Alex and Erica joined Cassie beside him.

"Congratulations, Dad!" Connor said.

Mark stared up at the sign, shaking his head in disbelief. "Did you have anything to do with this?"

"Maybe," Alex said.

"Kind of," Connor said.

"Yeah, they did," Cassie and Erica said.

Jennifer approached. "Doctor Hansen, the media is ready for you."

"Tell them I need some time with my sons," Mark said.

"It's cool, Dad," Connor said.

"Yeah, go ahead," Alex agreed.

"Okay. I'll see you at dinner," Mark said.

As Mark walked off with Jennifer, a sea of reporters and cameras engulfed them.

"Let's go on the Ferris wheel," Alex suggested.

There was a long wait for the Ferris wheel, but when Connor, Cassie, Alex, and Erica joined the end of the snaking queue, every single person who was waiting, stepped out of the way, gesturing for the four of them to go ahead, and calling them heroes. Over the past few weeks, life at the hospital had been better than ever before. And everyone—the doctors, hospital staff, even many of the patients—knew why. The news media had seen to that.

When they arrived at the front of the line, Alex turned to Connor. "You first, bro."

Cassie and Connor stepped into the open car, and the ride attendant shut the door. The car began to climb. Higher and higher. Above the sea of people. It didn't stop until it reached the very top.

As the car swung gently, Cassie looked into Connor's eyes. They hadn't kissed since that one very tentative kiss on the roof, but Connor was sure that Cassie wanted to kiss him now. And he wanted to kiss her too. More than anything.

Cassie leaned toward him. Connor's heart raced.

He closed his eyes.

* * * * *

ALSO BY J.W. LYNNE

THE UNKNOWN
Eight children are kidnapped in the night and wake up in a mysterious world full of secrets.

WILD ANIMAL SCHOOL
A teen spends an unforgettable summer caring for elephants, tigers, bears, leopards, and lions at an exotic animal ranch.

ABOVE THE SKY
Teens uncover the truth in a society founded on lies.